WITCH BOUND

A PACK BOUND SERIES PREQUEL NOVELLA

LEISL LEIGHTON

PERMIEN PRESS

Published by Leisl Leighton (as Permien Press). For more information, email: leisl@leislleighton.com

First Published 2020 in *Fantasy Realms Anthology: Warlords, Witches & Wolves* © 2020

Re-edited and republished by Permian Press 2021

Cover design by Lana Pecherczyk; Edited by Brooke Halliwell of Brooke Review

 Formatted with Vellum

PRAISE FOR LEISL LEIGHTON

WITCH BOUND

To SuperDan and Wonder Woman Lana:
This book wouldn't have been written if not for you. Thanks for asking me
to write it.
This one's for you.

1

Paul Collins screamed.

He'd opened his mouth to laugh at his friend's joke, but instead, the scream flew out of his mouth. Not a yell, not a shout. A scream.

He tried to shut his mouth, but the sound continued. It went on and on, a high-pitched wailing noise that would shatter his guards' sensitive eardrums if he didn't stop it soon. But there was no stopping this noise. It kept coming, growing and growing until there was nothing but the scream.

He was no longer Paul Collins, warlock, seer, son of the too-weak Pack Witch, Morrigan Collins, and Pack McVale's singular hope for the future.

He *was* the scream.

A scream that echoed down through the vast channels of power that came to him from somewhere in the future, making him its bitch. Mortifying. Horrifying. Bringing him low until he was this ... this miserable destroyer of hope and love.

He glanced around as the scream continued. His guard—those who were supposed to be his friends—were down on the ground around him, their eardrums blown out, blood streaming from ears, nose, eyes and mouth. He wanted to help them, but he couldn't move. Could only kneel in the dirt where he'd fallen, his mouth open, the unearthly scream flying out to fill the sky and earth around him.

Leaves trembled in the eucalypts overhead.

The moon turned blood red.

The sky turned purple.

Warlock lightning—blue, green, orange, purple and a never before seen red—flashed all around him.

Purple wings in the sky, shrouding everything, hung over a pile of bodies—Were, witches, warlocks, humans.

And beyond, a terrible, oily darkness spread to cover it all.

They were dead. They were all dead. And he could do nothing to stop it.

No! No! Goddess, no!

He wanted to die. He wanted to die.

'Paul!"

Something touched his arm—a hand, soft and cool on his heated skin, fingers curling firmly, but not painfully. He stared down at it.

His name came again. 'Paul.' Such a sweet sound. Like a siren's call, it pulled him back, pulled him away from the black thoughts that crowded his mind. 'Paul? Are you okay?'

He blinked and *her* face swam in front of his eyes.

Ivy.

Panic speared through him as he took her in, standing there in her oversized fluoro t-shirt, big hoop earrings swinging against her neck and big eyes staring up at him in worry. She looked so fresh, so innocent, so unaffected and yet ... 'No. No. Go away. The scream. It will hurt you. Kill you. Just like it did all of them.'

She frowned her confusion as he gestured to the bodies of his guard lying on the ground.

Except, there were no bodies. His guard were staring at him as if he was crazy.

He *was* crazy.

2

And she'd seen it. Again. Every bloody horrible moment of his crazy. As crazy as his crazy mum.

'Fuck.'

'Paul.'

'Leave me alone.'

He shoved her hand away, her caring, her concern, and took off, away from their stares, their uncomfortable laughter and their attempts to make him feel better that would inevitably follow.

Not that Jackson and Luke and Stellan—the Were who'd been blood-bonded to him at his birth—would laugh at him like the others might. They were more used to his crazy and would fight to the death for him if he asked. They'd even fight their other pack mates to stop them from smothering their one remaining Pack Warlock with their concern. It was their job. Not that he'd ask them to ever do that.

Aunt Iris—more mother than aunt—had always taught him not to cause a fight within the pack. The Were could be hot blooded and formed cliques within the pack that were strong in a way witches and warlocks could not understand.

It was this that made them follow him now even though he'd made it clear he didn't want their company. He shoved up his defences against the pack bond so they couldn't track him through it and shoved all of his power into the one thought of escape.

Now.

The world swirled around him and for a sickening couple of seconds he was spinning through the void before he secured his intent and folded the void to his bidding. A tear opened and he stepped out onto a patch of soft, long grass where he collapsed, exhausted, miles away from where he'd just been.

He stared up at the sun, the long grass waving above him, silence all around except for one long, lonely howl that echoed in the distance.

Ivy. He'd hurt her. He hadn't meant to hurt her, but truthfully, it was for the best. She didn't want to get involved with someone as weak as he.

· · ·

IVY STARED at the place Paul had been, her hair blowing forward across her face in the little suck of wind he created with his transportation spell.

She rubbed her chest. Her wolf howled out loud at the ache—an ache that was growing every day. An ache that was partially hers but mostly his.

Why had he run from her? She knew he was embarrassed to be caught so lost to a vision, but she could help him. She knew she could. And yet, he wouldn't let anyone help let alone her.

It wasn't right. He was so lonely. So apart. Hurting. The maternal side of her—the wolf side of her—couldn't stand the pain emanating from him all the time. It had been growing steadily, but recently, it had got so much worse.

She had thought it was because of the visions he saw—so often of deaths and disasters to be averted, rarely anything happy or good. That would be enough to suck even the brightest of souls into a dark vortex.

But Paul's soul was still bright. So bright it blinded her the first time she saw it when she was still a pup and he a five-year-old boy coddled and kept apart from the pack except for those who were set to be his guards. She had felt drawn to him in a way her three-year-old mind could not understand. She'd never seen anyone like him. He glowed—white and blue and orange. And when his gaze had met hers as he glanced around over Pack Witch Iris's shoulder, he'd smiled and waved at her and she'd felt like the sun and moon had come out all at once. Bathed in the embrace of their light, it soothed and settled her more than she'd ever felt before, even with her mother and the other maternal wolves.

She hadn't known then what she knew now.

Paul was her mate.

Except, he barely knew she was alive. If he saw her at all, it was as the sister of one of his guard. Stellan, the big doofus, had spent so many years painting his little sister as a giant pain in his arse that Paul no doubt thought of her as the same. No, scratch that. She knew he did think of her as a pain in the arse. Look at the way he'd once again pushed her away and then left her behind.

Footsteps padded up behind her, reminding her she wasn't the only one Paul had left behind. She turned to look over her shoulder at Luke—their next Alpha if she was reading the signs correctly—Stellan and Jackson as they stared in frustration at the empty spot where Paul had just been.

'Man, I hate it when he does that.' Stellan kicked the ground. 'We're going to get in so much trouble.'

'Yeah,' Jackson snorted. 'Iris is going to be so pissed.'

'Forget Iris. My dad is going to rake us over the coals for not staying on his tail this time.' Luke blanched as he swayed on his feet and rubbed the back of his head. 'My ears are still ringing from the last blasting.'

Ivy spun around to glare at the three of them. They looked like they'd been cut out of the same magazine with their stone-washed denim, their jacket sleeves pushed up, constantly checking their frosted floppy hair a-la Duran Duran. It was late summer for Goddess's sake. Way too hot for denim and jackets. Pretentious gits. How could Paul be such good friends with them all? He was so opposite to them in every way. Kind and good and ... natural. Like the guy from the Last Starfighter movie she'd seen last week with Siobhan. He was cute. These guys were idiots. Especially her big brother.

'Why are you glaring at us like that, Ivy?' Stellan asked, flicking her hoop earring.

She batted his hand away. 'You are all unbelievable.'

'What? What did we do?' Stellan asked, stepping back, hands up. 'He's the one that ran away.'

'You should have stopped him,' she said, stamping her foot even though it made her look a petulant teenager. She was only a few years away from her majority, having left her teenage years behind last year.

'From transporting? How do you suggest we stop that? None of us has powers. Short of grabbing him before he left and knocking him unconscious, there was nothing we could do,' Luke said.

She glared at him, his reasoning making her even more furious with them. 'It's always down to violence with you lot, isn't it? What about talking to him? What about asking him what's wrong? What about not standing around staring like a bunch of shocked idiots when he has a vision and making him feel like he's a crazy loner creep.'

All three males blinked at her.

'But, we're not here to help him with his visions or talk to him about them. That's for Iris and Dad to do,' Luke finally said.

'Yeah. We're just his guard,' her brother added.

'And his friends,' she said, stepping forward and poking him in the chest. 'You're supposed to see a cry for help when it smacks you in the face and then backhands you across the head. He. Needed. You. To. Be. His. Friends. Today.' Punctuated with a finger jab in each of their too big puffed up muscly chests. Her finger hurt—Luke's chest was hard—but she didn't care, Goddess damn it.

A shit-eating smile plastered itself over her brother's idiot face. 'Is that what you were doing, Poison Ivy?'

Agh! She hated that name. But rather than letting him see how much his calling her that pissed her off, she put her hands on her hips and said, 'Yes. Because I'm a nice person who is concerned about our only Pack Warlock. I want to make his life easier, not harder, you morons. Maybe you should think of giving that a try.'

'But ...' Jackson said. 'We didn't do anything.'

'No, you didn't. And that's the problem.'

Jackson got a look on his face that made her want to slap him. 'I think your sister is sweet on the warlock, Stellan.'

'I think she is too, Jackson. Poison Ivy and the warlock sitting in a tree—'

The slap rang out in the air before she even knew she'd moved her hand. She stared at the imprint of her fingers on her brother's face, the shocked expression replaced by one of confused hurt that made her feel like an absolute dick. But then the expression morphed into one of embarrassed anger.

'What the fuck, Ivy,' he said, touching his cheek. 'How am I supposed to explain this to the parental units?'

Despite the fact he could be a know-it-all twenty-five-year-old git, she knew her brother wouldn't rat her out, even though he was embarrassed she'd smacked him one in front of his friends. She huffed out a laugh. 'As if. Besides, you deserved it.'

'Why? Because I sang a stupid ditty?'

'Yes. It's disrespectful to our Pack Warlock. Mum and Dad will tell you so and you'll be in more trouble than I would for hitting you.'

'I was just having a bit of fun.'

She glared at him. Fun to him, cruel to her. Not that he knew the full reason why. Not that he or anyone else could ever know the full reason why.

They'd tell her she must be wrong. They'd make sure she never let her wolf reach out to Paul and make the mating connection. They had plans for him. Plans that didn't include him mating with some maternal female. Years ago, she'd heard Iris and David—their Alpha —laying out their plans one night around the fire after they thought everyone else had gone to bed. But now it was no longer a secret. Everyone knew. They needed new witch blood to restart their coven. Iris and David had organised for Paul to meet various witches from other packs they were aligned with. There was talk that one of the Pack McClune witches was proving to be in the running for the binding. Powerful and talented, she was just the right choice to strengthen their pack and re-invigorate their strangely dwindling coven.

Her wolf growled at the thought of Paul loving someone else.

There's nothing we can do, she whispered to her wolf inside her mind. *It's for the good of the pack.*

She rubbed at her chest again, the ache throbbing anew even as her wolf subsided, knowing she was right.

She'd have to leave when Paul handfasted with the McClune witch. She couldn't stay around and watch the man who was meant to be her mate bond with someone else. Which he could do. A mating didn't work for the magical and humans in the same way it did for the

Were. They got to meet and date and fall in love and choose each other. He was not bound to her unless she pulled on those strings. But she had no right to pull on those strings.

For the good of the pack, she had to leave him alone.

Stellan, tossing his floppy fringe off his brow in that affected way that usually made her want to snort-laugh, was now complaining about what lie to tell everyone about the slap mark on his cheek. Rather than giving in to her maternal wolf's need to make him feel better, she let her pain have free rein and snapped, 'I don't know, Stellan. Maybe you should tell them Mary-Louisa didn't like the way you fondled her breasts. She hates the way you pinch her nipples, you know.'

And on the sound of a gasp and a burst of laughter from Luke and Jackson, she took off. She knew she'd be even faster if she pulled her change around her and gave in to her wolf's need to run free, but if Paul needed her to pull him out of a vision, he wouldn't be happy about it if she had no clothes on. Having lived with the pack all his life, she would have thought he'd be used to the casual nudity of the Were when they changed from wolf to their human form. But he always ran the other way when she made the change when he was around.

Her wolf scratched at her mind, understanding why she couldn't let it out to make the run, but offering a bit more of itself so she could run faster. She let her wolf slip its energy into her muscles a little more and picked up speed. One of the fastest runners in their pack, the only one who could catch her would be Luke, but he was still too busy laughing his arse off at her brother's shock and embarrassment.

Served him right.

Served them all right if they got in trouble for letting Paul go off like that.

Well, if they weren't going to look for him, she would. She might not be able to bond to him, but she could take care of him in the way her maternal side demanded. She would find him and make sure he was okay, even if she had to do so from afar.

She could still feel the ache of him inside her, pulling at her, showing her the way. Except, the ache had changed, had become desperate.

She ran faster. She had to get to him before the desperation pulled him even further into his dark funk. She wasn't sure what she could do for him, but she could make it so he didn't feel so alone. At least she could do that.

2

Aunt Iris would be truly angry he'd used his power to transport himself like that. *'Such a use of power was only to be used in extremis.'* Her words said to him on his eighteenth birthday as she'd taught him the spell that could save his life if anyone ever came after him.

Why they'd come after him, he had no idea. He was Pack McVale's last Pack Warlock and his aunt the last Pack Witch now his mother was dead, but when he married a witch from another coven as she and their Alpha planned, and had all the babies they'd plotted for, that fact wouldn't matter. Not that it mattered now. Nobody knew about the Were and their covens, and no other Were would come after him. The Were revered the witches and warlocks, even from rival packs.

They were all being ridiculously cautious. And if anyone would know, it was him. In all the years he'd been having visions, he'd seen no sign that anything was coming for him. Only the nightmare images of the future that made his life hell because he was somehow responsible for trying to figure out a way to avoid them.

Goddess, his head ached. Perhaps he shouldn't have transported straight after a vision. It was too late to worry about it now. He was here and glad of it. At least here nobody would be nagging at him to tell them about what he'd seen and make him go back in to try to figure it all out so they could change it.

He took a deep breath and let his gaze wander across the view. There was a reason this was his favourite spot to come to when he was stressed and uncertain. It was one of the best views to be had at Pack McVale's Red Hill base. Plus, nobody else ever came here.

This hill—his hill—rose above the undulating land of the grass and tree-covered hills, giving him a glimpse of the beach in the distance and the shining glimmer of blue water that spread out from the Peninsula to Tasmania. This part of packlands was given over to grazing cows and sheep, the vineyards and orchards on the inland side, and as a result was quieter and he could pretend he was on an island by himself, far from the hustle and bustle of pack life and the expectations placed on him.

But today, as he glanced around, as he breathed in the faint scent of salt and sun-warmed grass, the calm he needed seemed too far away.

He dropped his head into his hands and fought the need to cry. He couldn't go back yet. He couldn't go back into that vision like his aunt would require him to. He never wanted to see it again let alone furrow around in its dark depths trying to figure it out.

Hell. He wasn't strong enough to carry everything the pack needed him to. He had no idea how he'd gotten away with them not noticing this serious flaw in their lone warlock. But they had to start seeing the cracks sometime soon. It was inevitable. And when they did, disaster would follow. Because how could he expect any witch from another pack, even a kind and thoughtful one like Mariella from the McClune Coven, to handfast with him and help rebuild their coven and the strength of their pack?

He would end up being as much of a disappointment as his mother.

He swallowed hard and looked up, staring at the water in the bay. Usually its sparkle and endless undulation made him feel better. Today, it did nothing but make him thirsty.

He wished he'd thought to bring a bottle of water. He could conjure one, but he really had used up too much of his powers already and he'd get even more of a tongue-lashing if he completely drained himself of power.

He could always tap into the pack bond to top up. But then Aunt Iris would know and come looking for him and he wasn't up for one of her lectures. Especially given she would be even more angry that he'd tried to take power from the pack bond without asking permission to do so. *'There are consequences for everything we do. Taking power is an exchange, an agreement with the Goddess and the universe to allow us to change things from what is expected to what is not. There is punishment for taking that which we have not sought permission to use.'*

He'd heard that over and over again in his twenty-two years. What he wanted to ask her was if permission was so important, then why had nobody ever sought his permission to thrust these visions in his head? It was one big cosmic suck for him. Or he was one big cosmic sucker.

Maybe he should run away like his mother had. She'd taken off when she was eighteen and he was four years older than that now. A year shy of his 'wolf majority' when he would be pulled into the pack hierarchy and included in all important discussions about his life.

He'd been holding onto reaching that all important age for years, but right now, it seemed an eternity away. He wasn't sure how much more he could take of this.

He scrubbed at his face with the heel of his hand and sighing loudly, flopped back onto the soft grass behind him. It would all be far more bearable if he had happy visions as well as the dark ones. Or at least more visions he could do something about. Maybe then, he would be able to deal. Maybe he would be able to breathe. Maybe then he wouldn't feel so weak. So useless. So hopeless.

A breeze tickled through the fronds of grass above him, making them bend and brush over his face like a caress. A sound like the sweetest humming, wound around him.

He knew that touch, that sound.

'Goddess?' The grass caressed him again. He sat up, a thrill in his chest. She was here. Arianrhod. She'd not visited him for a while. Perhaps he could ask her. Surely she would know.

He crossed his legs and placed his hands on his knees, palms up to the sun, then closing his eyes, he sank into his mind, into the place where his magic was seated, where his gift connected to the aether and allowed him to cross into that place that most could not visit.

There was a hiss and a click, a sense of swirling and falling and then a small pop. The scent of salt and seaweed greeted him, along with the rumble of waves crashing on the beach. He opened his eyes.

Sand stretched, golden and sparkling, on either side of him as far as he could see. Behind him dunes rose to caress the base of cliffs so high they sailed up to touch the sky. At the top of those cliffs was a forest, ancient and green filled with trees and flowers coloured across the spectrum with scents gentle and sweet, to spicy and bold. She'd taken him up there a few times to watch over the turquoise, green and purple sea that shifted and rose in frothy waves as it stretched out to the horizon. He'd asked if he could stay here forever. She'd simply smiled and told him it wasn't his time. 'But you can visit to settle yourself when things get too bad.'

'Why will they get bad?'

'This too you will see.'

He had known she wasn't talking about getting older. She had meant that he would 'see'. The knowledge of that made him want to shout and rage at the universe for doing this to him.

He didn't want to see. He didn't want to be strange. To be other. To never fit in. He wanted to truly belong and not just because his position as last Pack Warlock of Pack McVale made him wanted, needed. Their desperate hope in him was a crushing weight that was killing him.

'Sulking again, Seer-boy?'

One of the waves had risen up in front of him, parted, and out of the green and purple water stepped his Goddess, Arianrhod.

He gasped as he always did upon seeing her. She was doing that shifting thing she did—a Goddess to so many races, she had the face of many. As she walked towards him, her skin shifted from palest white to olive to amber to darkest black and back again. Her eyes did the same, shifting across all the colours of the spectrum and filled with what looked like a galaxy of stars swirling at their centre rather than pupils. Her hair changed colours too—palest silver to golden blonde to red then darkening to auburn, brown and finally black. Always long and curling and twisting in the breeze that wove eternally around her, it writhed around shoulders bared by the halter-neck of the dress she wore—a dress that flowed down a form that made his gut twist uncomfortably and his skin prickle with awareness of just how fucking beautiful and desirable she was. She was the Goddess of Fecundity in one of her guises so had this effect on all, but she usually toned her sexuality down when she appeared to him.

She'd first come to him when he was a young boy, had held him to her bosom and stroked his hair, holding him like he wished his mother had held him and his aunt rarely did.

His aunt said it was to make him strong. He snorted. She'd failed there.

As the Goddess sauntered towards him, over the wet sand, water frothing at her feet, her cherry red lips twisted at the corner in a knowing smile, a deep dimple flashed in the groove of her cheek before it flashed to another visage and another then another.

His stomach flipped and swirled at the disconcertingly alien effect. 'Can you stop doing that?' he asked, waving at her ever-changing faces. He swallowed hard, hoping that he could stop himself from vomiting all over her beautifully manicured feet. Crazy visions, screaming in front of his friends uncontrollably before running away only to vomit all over the Goddess's feet. He was having a great day.

'Sorry,' she said, her expression showing her chagrin. 'I forget sometimes that it does that. Is this better?' Her features settled into the one that he'd become most familiar with—the Celtic Goddess of palest skin and fire-red hair, a bow strung over her back, her dress now the animal skins of an ancient huntress. Her eyes still shifted through a spectrum of colours, but he'd learned to deal with that oddity.

He nodded. 'Thanks.' The huntress was the easiest of her faces for him to be around—sensual with a frightening kind of fierceness that somehow made him feel protected. He relaxed a little. 'Thank you for answering me today.'

'I felt your need was great.' She nodded and took a seat beside him. She had never let him follow the formalities in this place—her anger a great and terrible thing if he tried to stand or hang his head in her presence. This place was for them both to relax and be themselves. At least that's what she'd told him when she'd first brought him here. He was not even allowed to call her Goddess here.

Here, she was Arianrhod and he was Paul and they were friends.

A strange kind of friendship, unequal in every respect from an outsider's point of view, but equal enough for them.

'Tell me what is troubling you, my young friend.'

He moved to hug his knees, staring out at the horizon, the crash of the waves a reflection of the troubles in his mind. He did not answer right away—he'd learned long ago trite answers were not appreciated. She told him this place was to help him sort through the worries in his mind and soul, but it would not work if he did not respect the process. After a long moment of staring, he rubbed his hand over his tired eyes. 'I am so sick of being alone.'

'You are never alone, my friend. There are many who are always around you.'

'I know. I'm always surrounded. Never left alone.'

'So, what is it you want? To be alone or not alone?'

He turned to look at her, her fine profile reflecting thoughts that were as equally troubled as his. 'I want to be wanted for me. Not because I have power. Not because my gift gives my pack an advantage. Not because of a status I was born into and didn't earn. I wish not to feel so weak all the time.'

She turned her gaze on him. His skin prickled in the face of the power that radiated off her at all times, but it was more intense when she looked at him with those all-seeing eyes. 'You are unhappy with your life.'

'Yes. How did you guess?'

Thankfully she didn't take offence at his sarcasm, just stared at him for an unnervingly long time, then asked, 'Why?'

He faced her, holding her gaze even as the extent of her powers punched into him. 'Because I didn't choose this. It happened to me. And there's nothing I can do about it.' He pointed to the waves. 'I might as well be a bit of flotsam on those waves, tossed and turned about, never having any say over where I'm going or even if I should sink or float. How can I live a lifetime of this?' He dug his fingers into the sand at his side, thumping his chin—a little painfully—onto his upraised knees. 'My mother was weak too, but at least she got to run away from it all.'

'You are not like your mother, Paul. And you cannot run away like she did.'

'And why is that exactly? Why could she live without the link and I cannot? There's something about that that just doesn't add up.'

She sighed. 'You know perfectly well, why.'

'I know what I've been told.'

'What you've been told is true. Your mother could live apart because she was never strong enough to connect to the pack. Her powers were never in danger of hurting her or others or exposing you all and therefore she did not need the pack bond to channel her powers into and survive. You, on the other hand, my seer-friend, are a different kettle of sea-dwellers.'

'Fish.'

'What?'

"Different kettle of fish' is the saying.' It was kind of satisfying how she got things like that wrong every now and then.

'Different kettle of fish. Yes.' She smiled and patted her knee. 'Different kettle of fish.' She faced him again with an abruptness that was startling, her smile fading. 'Your power can never do without the bond. You need it to survive. Your power would build and build until you lost control if you were unable to channel the excess power to the Were. Your power is even greater than your aunt's—greater than any witch or warlock seen in any pack for many hundreds of years.'

He snorted. 'I find that hard to believe. I am not strong. I am weak.'

'Weak in soul at the moment perhaps, but not weak in power. If you were to leave Pack McVale, you would die and you would take others with you. Not to mention that without you, your pack would be destroyed by the Curse.' She sighed and stared out at the ocean, a small frown creasing between her brows. 'Even if you did not care for your own life, you cannot endanger the life of others. It is not in your character to do so. And, despite the fact you feel so *other* from them most of the time, you would never be able to bring yourself to destroy your pack.'

'My pack wouldn't be destroyed if I was to die. My aunt is still alive. She could still bare children if she so wished. But she doesn't. She wants to lay all the burden of our future on me.'

The Goddess stared at him for a long moment until he looked away, unable to hold her gaze.

'Your aunt cannot have children. Like so many of those with the talent of spirit-talking, she is unable to procreate.'

Paul frowned. 'She never said.' But before he could feel sorry for her, he said, 'But even if that's true, she could still bind witches from other packs to ours to keep our coven going. It's been done before.'

'Not lightly done, as well you know. And other packs will not want to gift their coven members to Pack McVale when it is in danger of starting the Curse. If the pack is to survive, your line must survive. That means you must survive. There is no other choice.'

'Choice. There's the word of the moment. Even my weak, supposedly powerless mother got to choose what was best for her.'

'Your mother had to leave you all. I don't think it was much of a choice.'

He jerked around to stare at her. 'Not from where I stand. She got all the choice. She could have stayed but she chose to leave.' He sighed and dug his hands a little deeper into the sand, looking down, knowing he was being a whingeing fuck-head, but unable to stop. He was so tired. So sick and tired of it all. 'That's all I want. To have a choice that is mine. To know that Fate doesn't have its hand up my butt making my mouth and limbs move like some great big cosmic joke.'

'You are not a cosmic joke.'

He snorted, lifted the sand and let it drift through his fingers.

She put her hand on his shoulder—power spiked through him, making him go rigid with it, the sand in his hand sparking and turning to glass as the warlock lightning sprang into being on his fingertips. Despite the dangerous flare of power, she didn't let go as she usually would do. She did not even seem worried by the fact she was overloading him with power the human body and mind was not ready to accept. Was she angry with him? What had he said to make her so angry? 'Arianrhod?' he said through a clenched jaw, managing to turn his head towards her. There was no expression other than a sad expectation on her features. 'It's too much,' he managed.

She shook her head. 'No. It's not. You can deal with it. You can deal with so much more. You are not weak. You are strong. But you are right. You should not be doing this alone.' And so saying, she channelled even more power into him through her hand. He shuddered and cried out, the power firing through his synapses, sparking through his veins, firing his lungs. Oh fuck. Was she trying to burn him to death? To make him explode? He knew his body wasn't exactly here, but he was pretty bloody certain if he exploded here, he would explode in reality.

'What ... have ... I ... done?'

'Nothing. That is the problem.'

'What more can I do?' he yelled, his fury overtaking the pain she was causing, taking some of the power and feeding it back into her. She hissed—with pleasure or pain, he couldn't quite tell.

'That's it. See? You have so much more control than you think you do. You do not need my help.'

'Control? I don't have any control at all.'

'You do. But I don't need to show you. She will.'

Then he was thrust out of the dream-plane and he was falling.

3

Paul spun around. Was he still falling? His eyesight was fuzzy but there was something in front of him. He grabbed a hold of it.

'Ouch. Steady on, Paul.'

'Ivy?' He blinked to clear his vision. Her lovely face hovered over him, straight brows creased. 'What are you doing here? What happened?'

'Steady. Sit back down. There. Better.'

She lowered him back to the ground, soft grass tickling the bare part of his leg. 'Why are you here?'

She let go of his shoulders when he was sitting steady and sat beside him, close, but not close enough to touch. He missed her touch. It always soothed the sharp stabbing and burning pain that so often ran through his body—a symptom of his power and his visions. 'I followed you. I've been sitting guard, waiting for you to wake up.'

He shook his head slowly, closing his eyes, trying to make sense of her words. 'Why were you sitting guard?' He opened his eyes and looked around. 'What happened?'

She sighed and picked at a blade of grass, stripping it as she spoke. 'You had a vision. Earlier. Those dicks you call guards—'

He snorted a laugh. 'One of those dicks is your brother.'

'Still a dick.' She picked a little daisy and began to pluck its petals. Her wavy chestnut hair was pulled into a high ponytail, bits of it curling around her face and highlighting the arch of her neck. Unlike her peers, she barely wore any make-up, just a hint of something that highlighted her long eyelashes and a touch of frosted pink on her lips. She didn't need anything else. Her skin always held enough of a healthy glow, it didn't need make-up. She was so lovely.

She looked up at him, the topaz and green flecks in her hazel eyes glowing in the late afternoon light. He should look away, should actually leave like he usually did when he found himself alone with her, but he just couldn't make himself do it right now.

'... anyway, surprise-surprise,' she was saying, 'but they didn't think to go and get Iris when you came out of the vision unsteadily and instead let you take off.'

He raised his brows. He didn't remember the vision right now, only that thinking of it left a nasty taste in the back of his throat. It must have been a bad one. The ones he couldn't remember afterwards always were. And they were the worst ones to go back into later to figure out. Horrors slowly unfolding. One he didn't want to try to figure out now. Not with her by his side. She shouldn't be tainted by the darkness of his visions. She was too good. Too pure. A bright light that didn't need his darkness marring the gift of her.

He plucked at a daisy, mirroring her actions as he turned his thoughts back to her complaints about his guard. 'I told them I don't want them running to Iris every time I have a bad vision.'

'Maybe not, but they should have helped you, not stood around like dumb idiots when you took off.'

He frowned. 'Hang on. If I lost my guard, how come you found me?'

She looked down at the daisy she was plucking, her ponytail flipping down to cover the side of her face. 'I know you come here when you need some down time. I just guessed this was where you'd be.'

'Oh.' She'd guessed but his guard hadn't. How had she known? Why did she know? 'Have you been following me?'

She ducked her head down further, but he still saw the blush that crept up her neck. 'Not following. Not like stalker following anyway. Just … making sure you are okay. You feel so … sad. And alone. More than my wolf likes.'

'Your wolf worries about me?' His breath began to burn a little in his chest.

She glanced up at him, her glorious eyes spearing into him for a breathtaking moment before she ducked her head again, hoop earrings jangling against her neck, her t-shirt slipping further off her shoulder.

He swallowed hard. He shouldn't look. She was Stellan's sister. And she wasn't meant for him.

Thankfully she didn't see his struggle, her attention back on the daisy she was shredding, then in a voice he had to lean in to hear, said, 'My wolf has to know you're okay, okay?'

'Really?'

'Of course. She's a maternal wolf.'

'Yes. Of course.'

She didn't look up at him, her gaze firmly fixed on her hands.

His followed her gaze, watching as she pinched a hole in a daisy stem and pulled another one through. She had such beautiful hands. They weren't perfect princess hands—no, it was obvious she did hard work with those hands, working the vines and in the orchards when she wasn't helping in the kitchens or studying, part of the workforce that had made the McVale vineyards into the success they were today. Her nails were short, her thumb nail on her right hand bitten down, the skin there a little red-raw. She always chewed it when she was thinking deeply—which she did mostly when she was studying. He smiled as she lifted her hand and bit at her fingernail now. He wondered what she was thinking.

His gaze roamed over her, taking advantage of the fact she was studiously not looking at him.

Her long, tanned legs were crossed in front of her, her shorts showing off the length of her legs, the roundness of her hips.

His mouth went dry. Hell. He loved the curves of her. He'd had no idea how much until sitting here now with her, so close they were almost touching. He wanted to tell her so that she wouldn't be so self-conscious about those curves anymore, would stop wearing the over-sized t-shirts and baggy pants she liked to wear so much, crossing her arms over her body to hide her generous breasts.

Although, she wasn't wearing baggy pants today, just those short-shorts. They weren't hers he realised—they must be Siobhan's. The Were-soldier in training was always strutting around in clothing that was too tight and too short, hair too big, too many necklaces and bracelets on and make-up too brightly coloured, lecturing Ivy on her dress sense. Why Ivy chose today of all days to listen to her, he had no idea, but by the Goddess, it was driving him crazy, seeing that expanse of long tanned leg so close.

She hadn't furthered their conversation as to why she had come to find him. He would have left it there—should have left it there given the forbidden nature of his feelings for her—except some demon inside him made him say, 'What about you? The part of you that isn't wolf? Does it worry about me too?'

Her fingers stilled and he didn't think she was going to answer, but then she said, 'I like to know you're okay too. As a friend,' she said in a hurry. 'Like I worry about all of my friends.'

Friends? He'd done his best to ensure they weren't even that. Not easy to do given she was a maternal Were whose job it was to make certain everyone was cared for. And not easy to do when, despite his best efforts, he could never make himself fully disengage when others were around. He loved listening to her; often found himself drawn to her when they were in a group together, listening as she spoke to her friends about her hopes and dreams, her plans to finish her Bachelor in early childhood education and go on to do her Masters and even-tually a doctorate. She was so smart; he knew she'd do it. And ambi-tious in that gentle way of hers which he found so appealing. He'd heard her talk over with Siobhan her hopes and dreams for starting a cross-pack early childhood centre to promote connection and under-standing between the packs. He was fascinated in the idea. Wanted to talk through it with her. But of course, he couldn't. Even when she tried to engage with him, speaking to him in a way that made him feel welcomed and a part of everything in a way nobody else did, he had forced himself to walk away. He was surprised she didn't hate him or talk of him with disdain like she talked of her brother and his friends.

Maybe it was because he used to treat her like a friend—or his friend's kid-sister. He wished he could go back to those days when she'd been Stellan's baby sister and nothing more. But she'd been more than that ever since she'd graduated from school two years ago. He'd been unable to take his eyes off her in her flowing yellow dress, the crimson cap and gown bringing out the gold in her skin, the topaz in her eyes, her smile so wide and alive it stole his breath.

He swallowed hard thinking of it now.

Kind Ivy.

Beautiful Ivy.

Sexy Ivy.

Goddess, how he wanted her. He'd wanted her for so long, it was an ache inside. But it was no good. He was meant for another.

He tried, he tried so hard to think of his duty to the pack, to her, but he couldn't. Not with her sitting so close. Not with her telling him she wanted to make certain he was okay and looking at him with those eyes that said it was more than friendship she wanted fro—

His thoughts crashed to a halt. Wait. What? He looked at her, begging her in his mind to look up at him.

She did.

Their eyes clashed.

Passion. Longing. Aching need.

For him. She felt that for him.

How could he have missed something so monumental?

Memories of her crowded through his mind: Ivy laughing after winning a race with her best friends, her eyes lit up, her generous mouth open wide and uninhibited as her laughter sang to the sun, her glorious chestnut curls a riot around her heart-shaped face, the laughter stopping as her gaze met and clung to his; Ivy pulling herself out of the water at the beach, her toned curves and olive skin glowing golden in the sun, her hair slicked back, eyes pools of bliss as she stood, arms out, and enjoyed the warm breeze and the sun until she'd spun to see him and the others sitting there, her gaze meeting his before she'd blushed, grabbed a towel and run off; Ivy looking more at home than anyone had a right to be in his aunt's kitchen, cooking her famous zucchini bread—Goddess, he loved her zucchini bread! —and offering him a piece, telling him she'd cooked it just for him; Ivy sitting at a desk, nibbling at her nail, brow furrowed in deep thought as she read the text book before her, seemingly lost in her studies until she'd suddenly looked up at him with what he now recognised as a look of confused want and longing in her eyes.

A longing that went beyond sexual attraction. Went beyond the link of the pack bond. Went beyond the ties of friendship.

'Ivy?'

Her eyes widened. There was a tug as something pulled tight inside him, a click of realisation falling into place.

She made a sound, an oof of surprised recognition. 'Are you sure? It's not what they want. You can deny it.'

He nodded. 'I know. I've been trying. But I can't. Not anymore.'

'Neither can I.'

'Then yes?'

She smiled at him—the sun came out with her smile and it was blinding.

He held his hand out. She took it in hers. He tugged.

Then she was on his lap and they were kissing and he never wanted to come up for air. His hand was on her breast, her nipple pebbling against his palm. He rubbed his hand up and down and she moaned into his mouth, the sound vibrating down to his stomach, making his cock jerk, his balls tighten. He was afraid of spilling before getting her close to where he was, but as she cupped his face and pulled away to look into his eyes, he knew he would never do anything but make certain her life was bliss.

He ran his hands up her spine, pulling her closer as she pulled him closer. He dug his fingers into her hair, gently pulling it free from the ponytail, the soft silk of it twining around his fingers, his wrists.

His top tore—she had used her claws. He'd done that to her,

brought her so close to the edge that she couldn't hold back her wolf. He shouted his exhilaration up to the sky, feeling like a god, but she pulled his head down and took his mouth with hers.

The taste of her. It was like nectar, sweet and spicy all at once and something for which he'd never get his fill.

He tumbled back and her thick silky hair swung over his face, tickling his cheeks. He laughed. She laughed. So much joy. He had no idea there would be so much joy.

She sat up, took off her t-shirt, her high breasts encased in fine white cotton with little flowers printed on it. So beautiful. So Ivy.

She blushed under his gaze, but it was a good kind of blush, not self-conscious, but full of a sense of herself, her worth, and how she was so god-damned sexy to him, with him.

He reached for the button on her shorts—

The earth began to spin around and around and around.

No. No. Not now. But he couldn't stop it. The vision flew towards him with earth-shattering force.

He heard her calling out, calling his name, but he couldn't answer, instead saw Ivy standing with him before the pack, their Alpha declaring them mates, equal expressions of joy and concern crowded around them; he saw Ivy racing before him to their car, shouting at him that he had to hurry because she wanted to start their honeymoon right now then she was in the front seat of that car, her eyes wide as she cried out to him to watch out then they were rolling and rolling and the car exploded and they were gone.

The vision flipped.

They were now on a boat; a storm came up suddenly. The boat capsized, catching them in the rigging and they both drowned.

It flipped again to show them in the kitchen. There was a faulty appliance. He got electrocuted and as he died, Ivy fell next to him, as dead as her mate.

Over and over again, images after images of possible futures before them and in every one, they ended up dead.

Ivy was dead.

His mate was dead.

How could this be happening?

'Paul!"

He jolted upright, clutching his head, yelling, 'No. No. No.'

Ivy was dead.

Because he'd completed the mating bond, he'd caused her death. Over and over. He shoved into the visions, looked at the path, looked at ways to change the path that led to death, but there were none. Not one. If she mated to him, she would die.

He snapped out of the vision, scrambled to his feet, shaking his head. No, not just his head. His whole body was shaking. 'No. Not going to happen. I'm not going to do it. You can't make me.'

'Paul?' She stood, her hands outstretched, the hurt in her eyes a dagger in his heart. 'What's wrong? Tell me what's wrong?'

He couldn't tell her. Except, he couldn't stand the way her face was crumbling, the hurt he could feel inside her through the tenuous link of the mating bond—a bond that he had to stop in its tracks if he could. He put up a block, clamping down on those tenuous threads, attempting to crush them with his magic. But it was too late. They'd already gone too far.

'Ivy ... I ...' Goddess, he didn't want to cause her pain—which he would do if he stopped the mating in its tracks. It was too much. Too much. 'Goddess, please, help me.'

'You do not need me to help you.' Arianrhod's voice echoed through his mind reminding him of what she'd just said to him in the vision place.

He kept backing away from Ivy. She didn't move towards him, but her hand was stretched out and he could feel her pain and confusion pounding into him through the mating bond despite his efforts to block it with his powers. 'Make it all go away,' he shouted at the Goddess.

'I cannot make your destiny go away. Only you have the power to do that.'

He could change the future. He'd done it before. Many a time. Simply by telling others what he saw and helping them avert what fate might bring their way. But there were some futures that could not be changed; they were fixed points. If he mated with Ivy, she would die. He was as certain of that as he was of his next breath. He'd never changed a fixed point before. Didn't know it was possible. 'How?'

'You are a seer, a time-walker, a thread-puller. You have always had the power—you simply need to use it.'

He reeled. He'd never thought of his power like that. 'What do I do?'

'Break the thread you don't like. See a different thread and weave it into your story.'

'You make it sound easy.'

'You've broken small ones before. This is just a bigger thread. One that carries more weight and meaning certainly, but it can be broken like any other. Just be warned, though, break this thread and it carries consequences you may not like.'

He didn't care. If it saved Ivy, he would do anything, take any punishment that might come his way.

He opened his mind's-eye into his powers, saw the threads, found the one he wanted and pulled.

Even as he did so, he knew it wasn't going to be enough. He had to change everything. He had to make certain Ivy never remembered looking at him and even thinking 'friend'.

His soul cried out as he gathered the power to change even more of what Fate had woven.

Ivy screamed, the sound viciously painful and full of grief as he tore from her the future that could have been theirs.

Her scream killed even the tiniest bright spark of light he'd had inside him that was her presence in his life.

He grabbed another thread and tore it, manipulated it to change. Ivy's scream cut off and she collapsed into the long grass in front of him.

He wanted to take her in his arms, to hold her and whisper how sorry he was, but he still had work to do.

To save Ivy, he had to press on.

He held onto that knowledge as he changed past, present and future, turning his life into a literal living hell.

4

A cry caught in Ivy's throat, but she stopped it before it could come out.

There was something wet on her face. She lifted her hand and brushed it away—a tear. Many tears.

She'd been crying? Why had she been crying? And what was the feeling deep inside her, like something was missing?

'Hey, Poison Ivy. Stop standing there like a toad on a log and dance. It's a celebration. Come on.'

Stellan grabbed her and jerked her forward into the Dance circle, spinning her around and around. Laughing faces whirled by her as her brother danced her around the circle and back, their clapping and cheering rising in the air with the music and the snap and crackle of the bonfire at the centre of the circle.

What?

How had she got here?

Why were they dancing?

What was being celebrated?

A louder cheer rose and Stellan whipped her around, taking her off her feet before planting her back down again. Only his arms around her kept her from stumbling.

'You okay?'

'Y... yes.'

'Sorry. I'll be more careful.' He looked contrite. Her brother contrite? And considerate? What the hell was going on? She looked down and saw she was wearing her favourite spring-green summer dress with the spaghetti straps, tight bodice and buttons up the front of the long, flowing skirt. It was the dress she usually wore to pack celebrations.

He turned her around and she saw the two pack mates in the centre of the circle, their arms wrapped around each other, kissing.

A mating ceremony. She was at a mating ceremony? Whose?

The couple pulled back from their kiss, laughing into each other's faces.

Siobhan.

Her best friend's hair was extra-big and freshly tipped, earrings that could have played the role of chandelier hanging from her ears. She had on a tight black dress ruched at the sides, her favourite yellow leather jacket with fringing and six-inch black ankle boots that made her long legs look even longer. When had she bought those? And why had she gone shopping without her bestie?

As Siobhan turned towards her, Ivy saw she had her going out make-up on—green eyeshadow, black lashes, cheeks highlighted by slashes of rose blush and lips vibrantly pink. Under all the make-up and fancy clothes, she vibrated happiness, such happiness it was almost hard to watch.

Ivy rubbed at the ache in her chest. An ache that had edges to it, a horrible thought sliding into her mind—I will never have that.

She pushed the thought away. She wasn't jealous of her friend. She would never be jealous of another person's happiness—but why did that happiness make her feel so horribly sad?

Siobhan's new mate turned and howled into the night sky, revealing who it was.

Chloe. The apprentice to their Pack Librarian, she was six years their senior. The last Ivy had heard, Chloe was travelling through Europe and the British Isles talking to other packs and covens to gather data and see if they'd experienced the same slowing of births and increase in deaths that Pack McVale had been for the last thirty years.

Now she was apparently back here, wearing a beautiful white cheongsam with blossom print—a legacy of her mother's heritage—her black hair cut into a straight bob and looking as blissfully happy as Siobhan.

They were mated? Why the hell couldn't she remember Siobhan meeting the older female Were and mating to her? Surely that would have been something she would have had a front row ticket to?

She rubbed at her throbbing head. What had happened? Maybe she'd drunk too much of her father's delicious 1975 Cab Sav? Although, this didn't quite feel like that kind of headache.

Siobhan saw her and waved her forward. 'Ivy. Come make your speech.'

Ivy froze. Speech? What speech?

'Time for your best-friend speech, Poison Ivy,' Stellan said, pushing her forward.

She turned to slap at him, but he danced back and out of the way, almost slamming into Paul Collins who stood just outside the circle, hands shoved into the pockets of his dark blue suit pants, his white shirt highlighting his rangy, muscular frame and the width of his shoulders.

Something horrible curled in her chest at the sight of him. At the sight of that arrogant look on his aristocratic face as he watched her stumble forward. Was he enjoying her confusion? Her embarrassment as the crowd screamed her name to come take her part in the pack's acceptance of the mating? She hated him. He was the one who had started the nickname Poison Ivy that Stellan and his friends loved to tease her with.

She just wished he'd shut his big, arrogant, smart-arse mouth and stick with bleating his prophecies like a male Cassandra.

She shook her head. No, she didn't wish that, truly. She wasn't mean enough to wish the horror of his prophecies on anyone, even on the bane of her existence.

Why was he staring at her like that now? He looked almost curious? Or worried. Did he not think her capable of giving a speech of welcoming and acceptance for her friend and her mate? She'd show him.

She marched forward, anger buoying her, filling her with courage in the face of possible public humiliation. She'd never liked making a spectacle of herself, hated public speaking. But this was different. This was for Siobhan and Chloe. She could do this.

Walking up to the newly-mated couple, she took her place between them, holding out her hand. Siobhan put her hand on Ivy's first then Chloe followed and Ivy encased both hands by placing her other hand on top of theirs signifying their togetherness, their acceptance within the pack, and unity of the whole, echoing what the Alpha must have done earlier when accepting the mating into Pack McVale and starting this celebration.

Siobhan leaned in and whispered to her, 'I'm so glad you are here. I was worried you wouldn't make it.'

Ivy jerked to look at her friend. 'I'd pull myself out of my death bed to be here with you.'

'Don't joke about that,' she said, a cloud shivering across Siobhan's expression before she grabbed Ivy up into a fierce hug. 'I love you.'

'I love you too.'

Siobhan let her go before she could ask her what all that was about, and lifted her arms, the fringes of her jacket swishing around her. 'Quiet everyone. Let Ivy speak.' She took Ivy's hand again and suddenly everyone was looking at her with expectation.

Ivy didn't know what she was going to say—she still couldn't remember this mating taking place—but she opened her mouth and hoped for the best, leaning on the traditional blessing of welcome from a maternal Were to a newly-mated couple. As she spoke the blessing, she watched Siobhan and Chloe's faces as they stared at each other. She had a feeling they barely heard or saw anything around them as they smiled secretly at each other. Ivy stumbled over her words—the sexual energy between them was off the charts, blazing into her so strongly she couldn't help but blush. Wow. They seriously needed to get a room.

Everyone around her laughed and Siobhan knocked her shoulder against Ivy's, her face aflame, but humour and happiness in her eyes. 'Ivy!" she said.

Ivy realised she must have spoken the last words aloud. Rather than let her true embarrassment show, she took a ticket from her friend's usual moxy and beamed at her. 'This kind of feeling between a mated pair can only mean good things if I'm feeling it this strongly. And nobody deserves this happiness more than you two. I wish you happiness and peace and the blessing of the Goddess upon you. Only, when you have children, can I request you not use Stellan as a sperm donor. I can't think of anything worse than my brother's spawn growing inside my best friend.' Everyone howled with laughter as Stellan's growl of protest rumbled through the night.

'I'll get you back for that, Poison Ivy.'

She waved her hand at him. 'Yeah-yeah. You wish. Now let's get this mating ceremony finished so these two can retire to their home before they make me combust with their lust.' More laughter burst into the air as she grabbed first Siobhan then Chloe into a hug, then she stepped back, ceding the floor to Chloe's best friend, Megan.

She sighted her parents and went to stand next to them rather than with Stellan who was on the opposite side. She received their hugs and stood between them, her father's arm slung around her shoulders, while her mother linked their arms. Their actions settled her in a way nothing else could.

Nothing else except ...

Her gaze slid to Paul. He'd drawn closer to the circle and was standing just to the right behind Stellan, his face now lit by the flames of the torches marking the circle and the bonfire in the middle. He wasn't watching the mating ceremony.

He was watching her.

She shivered, the shiver prickling to centre in her core, clenching there.

Her mother shot her a look. 'Are you okay?'

'Fine,' she muttered.

'Are you cold?' her father asked, hugging her to him, her mother moving in closer on her other side, her hand now rubbing up and down Ivy's back.

'No.' The night had the chill of early autumn on it, a cool breeze blowing up from the ocean that hid beyond the cliffs at the edge of their packlands only a kilometre away, but she'd been dancing and what with the fire and the bodies crowded around, she was hot rather than cold. 'I'm actually a bit overheated I think.'

Her parents backed off a little, shooting concerned looks her way.

'I knew we shouldn't have let you dance with Stellan for so long. Let me go get you a drink to cool you down.'

'Some water would be nice.' Her throat was rather dry.

Callum McVale slipped away and out of the circle.

She stood beside her mother, still arm in arm and tried to concentrate on the ceremony in the centre of the circle and the happiness of her friend.

She was so happy for Siobhan. She'd been so worried about her friend lately. Siobhan loved her soldier training, but she'd been unable to settle to anything else and had become a bit wild when she wasn't training and taking a guard shift.

But now—she'd never seen her friend more settled. Maybe this was what she was waiting for, the final piece in the puzzle to make her life exactly how she needed it to be.

It was what every Were dreamed of—right?

She rubbed at her chest, the ache pulsing there now.

Her gaze slid across the pack circle again.

Paul was staring at her, a look of worry on his face.

But why was he looking at her like that? There was no reason to worry about her—other than the fact she seemed to have lost a bit of her memory. Had she been sick? But if so, then why was she here celebrating? It didn't really make sense. Nobody else seemed concerned though. Maybe she really had drunk too much wine. Siobhan was likely to have been in celebration mode since mating and had undoubtedly dragged her along to celebrate with her and Chloe.

Yes, that's what it must be. She was feeling rather tired all of a sudden. And her head really did ache. Now she was out of the lime-light, she had to admit her head was beginning to thump rather nastily. And the ache in her chest she'd noted before was sharpening, not getting better.

Her gaze skittered to Paul Collins again. He was still looking at her with those piercing blue eyes of his. Blue eyes that reminded her of the electric blue colour of glacial lakes, a colour that had filled her heart with so much joy when she'd first seen it on a trip to visit a New Zealand pack her family had ties with ten years ago. She'd thought back then of Paul's eyes.

If only they weren't always filled with such arrogance and disdain when looking at her.

Her wolf whimpered in her mind, its claws scratching under her skin.

Shh, girl. She hated it when her wolf was unhappy. *We'll slip away as soon as the happy couple are gone.*

Her wolf pushed at her, impatient.

She rubbed at the ache in her chest. She knew what her wolf wanted. *I promise we'll go for a run.* After she'd taken something for this headache that was getting worse with every moment.

Her mother touched Ivy's cheek. 'Go take a moment, beautiful girl. I left some headache remedy sitting on the kitchen bench.'

She stared at her mother—how did she always know? But her embarrassment over her mother knowing she'd partied too hard the last few days didn't stick. Her mother's maternal empathy was just too all-encompassing.

Rose McVale, one of the strongest maternal wolves in the pack, took her daughter's face in both her hands and kissed her nose. 'Go, take care of that headache. You've done your duty. Siobhan knows you haven't been well. She won't mind if you slip away.'

Ah, so she had been ill, not partying. That did explain her fuzzy memory.

'Besides,' her mother continued. 'They're about to slip away too after the speeches by the look of things, so you definitely won't be missed. So go. We don't want you having another collapse.' She smoothed her hand over Ivy's wild curls. 'You need to take better care of yourself. You've been working way too hard.'

'I've got things to accomplish, Mama.' She had to find some way to bring something special to the pack. She couldn't continue to be average in every way.

'I know, my driven girl. We're all so proud. But working hard does no good if all you do is drive yourself into the ground. Okay?' Another kiss, this time to one cheek then another. 'Now go.'

Ivy almost melted under her mother's caring, but her head was pounding and her chest was aching, and even though she would have lingered to hug her mother for longer, she gave Rose McVale a quick kiss and slipped away into the darkness towards the building that was her family's private home.

5

Ivy swallowed her mother's headache remedy. She sighed in relief as the healing powers Abby, the pack healer, had woven into the liquid took immediate effect.

She took another spoonful before putting the large bottle down. She frowned at the bottle. Why was it so large? Usually her mother and Abby didn't make this in such large batches because it had a short shelf life. It was half empty. Was this because she'd been sick? And just how long had she been sick?

She glanced at the calendar hanging on the wall beside the pantry. The dates were crossed off up to March 29th.

It was March 29th? But the last day she remembered was February 28th.

She gripped the bench, her wolf whimpering inside. She'd been sick for a month? Were never fell sick like that, their immune systems managing to fight off most things, but if not, changing into their wolves usually took care of the general round of bugs and viruses.

What the hell had happened?

She tried to search her memory for a clue—what was the last thing she'd done?

It was shrouded in thick fog, couldn't remember what had

happened. There was a whisper of her having been studying and then getting up because she felt something—an anguish or a pain—then, nothing.

Had she collapsed? And why had she suddenly come back into her head in the middle of the mating ceremony? Surely if she'd still been sick, her parents would have made her stay at home. So she must have been well enough and communicating for them to allow her to go. Not only go, but dance with her brother and stand up and give a speech.

But what had happened to her that she couldn't remember anything up until Stellan grabbed her and made her dance?

A month. Gone.

Hell.

She glanced at the calendar again, but the date was the same as it had been the last time she looked.

The date!

Uni! She'd only just started back. Now she'd missed a month of it? She'd never missed a day of school or uni in her life. How was she going to catch up?

Oh Goddess, she felt sick.

She clutched her stomach and ran to the loo, getting there just in time to heave up all the food she couldn't remember eating at the mating celebration.

When she was finally done, she stayed on her knees, gasping and shivering.

Was she still sick? Perhaps she should go to bed.

Her wolf whimpered again in her mind, pawing at her.

Shh girl. I know. She couldn't go back to bed—by all accounts, they'd spent too much time there already. Besides, even though she'd just thrown up, there was an itch under her skin, a need for wide open spaces and speed, the freshness of the ocean breeze across her face and tangling in her hair. It shoved away any weakness she felt, becoming an energised prickling in her skin, her muscles, her bones.

Yes. They needed to get outside and run. Running had always cleared her head—maybe that's exactly what she needed to do right now to remember anything of what had happened to her. And to figure out what she was going to do about uni.

She went to her bedroom, slipped out of her shoes, dress and undies, took off her earrings then gathered her change around her.

Rainbow glow lit the room and then she was seeing everything through her wolf's eyes, the night brighter, the air full of more scents, enticing her out the door. She trotted through the house and slipped out through the sliding glass door she'd left open and into the cool of the night, her thick tawny coat keeping her warm against the chill now in the air. Laughter and cheers and the warm glow of the fires from the pack circle were off to her left. She headed right towards the cliffs and the ocean.

She ran fast and hard, her paws slapping against the hard-packed earth as she took off up the road to begin with, then veered into one of the fields that had been given over to the apple trees that grew so well down here. The McVales were well known for their wine, but thanks to a forward-thinking Alpha, they had begun to diversify and were now investing in apple and cherry orchards. Cherry season was well and truly over, but the boughs of the apple trees around her were heavy with fruit. Normally she would have stopped and picked a few of her favourites—golden delicious—but didn't want to stop. Couldn't stop. She had to run. And run. It was the only thing that made sense right now.

She ran to the edge of the cliffs and down the path that led to the private beach that Pack McVale used year round. There was only a sliver of sand—the tide was riding high—but she ran along it, splashing through the waves as they rolled up the beach, enjoying the salty spray against her nose and paws. She ran to the far end of the beach and then turned and ran back the way she came. The water was lapping up closer and closer to the cliff, so she couldn't stay down here for long, but she knew she could make it to the other side of the bay that was theirs and back to the steps before running became swimming.

It was a close call, but she leaped up onto the first steps as the waves slapped up against the base of the cliff, building with each surge. She stood there for a moment, chest heaving, tongue lolling, and breathed the night in. She felt calmer and no longer like her life had been torn apart by some unseen hand against her bidding. A run and the ocean always fixed things. It was why she so loved it here, why she thought herself so lucky to have grown up here on the main McVale packlands. She loved going to uni but she so missed this when she was away. But soon—the end of this year—she'd be finished her Bachelor and could start on the plans she'd discussed with the Alpha, David, only the other day.

She frowned. No, not the other day. Over a month ago.

She huffed a sigh, the sound coming out of her snout like a snort.

Waves splashed at her feet, their spray hitting her in the face. She danced up a few steps, surprised by how high the ocean had got—she must have been here for longer than she thought.

Sighing again, she turned and padded up the stairs, wondering if the celebration was still going full tilt. By the look of the position of the stars and the moon in the sky, a few hours had passed since she'd headed out for her run. Her headache had thankfully not made a return visit, but as she ascended the stairs from the beach, she became aware of the strange sensation still in her chest. She'd not noticed it when running—too busy pulling oxygen into her lungs so she could keep going.

But now she was only walking, she couldn't ignore it.

Was there something wrong with her heart? Was that what had happened to her? Were rarely got sick from bugs and viruses, and their bodies were less likely to fall prey to diseases like cancer or neurological and heart issues, but that didn't mean it didn't happen.

Something wrong with her heart was the only thing she could think of to explain a month of illness, the large bottle of pain medication prepared by the pack healer at her house, her parents' worry and protectiveness—even Siobhan's words to her when she called her up to make a speech.

It was also the only reason she could think of that would explain this odd feeling of weakness and bruising ache in her chest, as if something incredibly important was now missing.

Should she have been running? She stopped as she reached the top of the cliffs and looked back. She was no longer panting heavily—hadn't felt more exerted than she usually would after such a wild run. And she felt much better than she had before she'd started her run.

Okay, so running seemed okay.

But standing around wondering what was wrong with her wasn't going to give her the information she needed to help her in the days ahead. She needed to wolf-up and ask her parents what had happened to her and admit she couldn't remember the last four weeks.

Although, did she really want to worry them more than they already were? The news that she couldn't remember anything since late February possibly wouldn't go down too well. Maybe she needed to ask someone else.

Siobhan was going to be too busy tonight, so her best friend was out.

Same for her brother—she'd seen him eyeing off Charlotte, the female Were eagerly returning his 'let's have us some sex' vibes. Maybe she should find Abby. As pack healer, she would be the best person to ask about the illness that had laid her low for such a long time. And Abby was probably the only one who could help her figure out why she couldn't remember anything of that time and maybe even enable her to gain back some of the memories.

It was a really horrible thing to know there was a gap in your mind.

She padded off across the field that bounded the edge of the cliffs, the long grass brushing against her fur, then headed up the hill between the apple trees before veering into one of the vineyards as a shortcut to where the Alpha house sat, the healer cottage beside it.

The noise of pack mates still celebrating drifted through the night, making her wolf prick up her ears over the happy sounds, a little surprised that it was still so loud. By this time, usually at least half the pack must have already retired for the night, but it had been too long between mating celebrations, so she expected they were all taking advantage of the good news. Not to mention the love that ran through the pack bond from the happy couple. There would be more than a few pack mates coupling up tonight to rid themselves of the wildness of that sexual energy.

A sexual energy that was so vibrant, it sang through her as she got closer, almost making her want to break her staunch rule of staying single and keeping out of the kinds of relationship messes Siobhan and others of their age seemed to fall into at the drop of a hat. Her wolf didn't urge her to give in though—she understood the need to keep themselves concentrated on their goals. But still, she couldn't help but close her eyes and enjoy the thrilling intensity of sexual awareness that pushed at her.

Damn, but she was so happy for her friend. To have found the one to share that with—it was every Were's dream.

Except hers. She didn't think she ever wanted to give herself over to someone that much. She was too much her own Were to want to have to fit someone else into her life. Had too much to prove to herself and the pack. Too much to accomplish.

But still, she was happy for those who found it, even if she didn't want it for herself.

A pulse of ache pulled at her chest and almost made her stumble.

Was her heart about to go? Was she having a heart attack?

She needed to get to Abby. She headed towards the pack circle— it was likely the pack healer was still there, using her healing abilities to make certain nobody got too exuberant, or if they did, be on tap to heal them immediately.

As she hurried up the slope towards the noise and the golden glow of flames from the torches and bonfire, the ache in her chest grew, pulling, tugging, making her gasp.

Such agony. Such sorrow. Such grief.

What the hell?

Then she saw him. And knew.

These weren't her feelings of agony, of sorrow and grief.

They were his.

Paul Collins.

Her nemesis.

The man whose gaze hadn't left her tonight as she'd danced with her brother then given her speech, and not for the entire time she'd stood with her parents.

He was standing against the wall of the apple storage barn overlooking the orchard. His blue eyes—glowing in her wolf night-vision—were on her once again.

As he watched her, that agonising ache inside him of sorrow and grief, grew and grew until she could barely stand it.

He was in pain. So much pain.

She had to help him.

She gathered her change—his need and pain so great she didn't care that she'd be naked before him like she usually did—but before the rainbow glow brightened more than a few centimetres around her, there was a buzz of energy and he was gone.

6

Ivy could still feel Paul's grief even after he vanished.

Oh Goddess. Such tearing loss. It was a thickness in the air around her. A painful grip on her heart, her lungs.

She had to do something. To help him.

But how could she do anything when he kept transporting himself away?

She frowned. Kept transporting himself away? Why would she think that? He'd never transported himself away from her before. He'd always made some sarcastic comment about her, laughing at her with his friends. He hadn't had to walk away because she was the one running away, tears in her eyes. She'd never been able to figure out what she'd done to make their Pack Warlock treat her with such disdain, never been able to stop it from hurting so much. More than when her stupid brother and the rest of their friends treated her like a pain in the arse.

Paul had never fled from her before. He wasn't the running away type. Too arrogant. And why not? He was their only Pack Warlock, their hope for the future health of the pack. He'd been spoiled rotten from the moment he'd been born, given every advantage, treated like a god almost. He was set to marry a strong witch from Pack McClune to keep the Collins line going. He had everything going for him.

So why had he run from her tonight? Why was he in such pain? Had anyone else noticed? Should she bring it to Iris and Abby's attention?

Surely they would have felt it. She was being arrogant to think they hadn't. They were so much more attuned to the pack and its members than she. She was only a maternal wolf after all. And not even one of the strong ones. Just average.

She turned from her path and headed back to her home. But with every step, heaviness enshrouded her until she was almost staggering under its weight as she let herself inside.

What the hell was happening? How could she feel this way? And why was she still feeling it so strongly?

Something horrible must have happened to Paul in the time she'd been unconscious and nobody had told her. Maybe nobody had wanted to upset her. Had the witch he was supposed to bind with died? She hadn't thought he'd been in love with her, but maybe he had been.

Hell.

Had he lost the love of his life? It hurt her to think that might be true. Perhaps she should go and tell Abby and Iris what she'd felt. It was possible they didn't know the full extent of his pain. He could be hiding it from everyone, not wanting them to see him in pain. He probably thought it a weakness. Idiot. Stubborn idiot. He was as stubborn as the stubbornest wolf.

But she'd caught him out tonight when he'd probably thought nobody was around and he could let down his guard. It's probably why he'd transported himself away—shock and shame.

Didn't the idiot know there was nothing to be ashamed of in grieving for a lost love?

Abby and Iris would be able to help him.

But instead of heading back to the pack circle to find them and tell them what had happened, she found herself running home to pull on some jeans and a jumper then grabbing the keys for the family's 4WD.

She drove along the orchard road, past the hills of vines and to the tallest hill that lay at the centre of the McVale packlands. She had no idea why she was heading this way, only that she felt drawn to it.

Her heart pulsed as she turned off the road, opened the gate into Hill Paddock, and drove up the steep rise, bumping along through the tall grass.

Something made her stop before she got to the top. She turned the car off then hurried up to the crest. There he was limned by the moonlight glowing from above. His head was bowed, hands over his face, shoulders hunched.

She'd never seen him look so small. So ... unguarded. So raw.

She watched him for a moment before moving towards him, quietly, carefully.

He didn't look up at her but he must have heard her coming—he had to at least have heard the 4WD.

Didn't he care that he was found? That she was there and could see him like this?

Perhaps he was having a vision? But she'd seen him have visions before and they didn't look like this.

Worry jagged up another notch and she ran the last few metres towards him. 'Paul. Paul. What's wrong? Why do you feel like this? Did you lose her? Is she dead?' She went down beside him, her arms around him before she could give it a second thought. He stiffened under her touch. She held on tighter. 'It's okay, Paul. You need help. Let me help.'

For a brief moment, he softened into her, his hands clenching on her back, but then he pushed away, scrabbling to a stand. 'No. No, you can't help. You are the last one who can help. You need to go.'

'What?' She stared up at him. He was right. She was the last one who should or could help him. Except, she was the only one here. And even though his attitude hurt and made her angry, she couldn't leave a pack mate alone when they were hurting like this. 'Don't be a stubborn arse, Paul.' She pushed to her feet. 'I can feel your pain. I know you need help. Why won't you ask for it?'

'You don't understand. You can't understand.'

'Why? Because I've never been in love? Because I haven't lost someone I love?'

He staggered back a step as if she'd punched him. 'What?' he said, his voice a breathy thread. 'How do you know?'

She took a small step towards him—oh Goddess, his pain was throbbing through her, making her throat thick. 'You lost her. I didn't know you loved her. I'm so sorry. So sorry.'

'What? What are you talking about?'

'Mariella? The McClune witch. The one you were to bond with. She's died, hasn't she?'

'No. Why would you think that?'

She blinked at him for a long moment then said slowly, 'But it's the only reason why you'd feel such grief. Losing someone you loved deeply. Like a mate.'

'I'm not grieving. You're wrong.'

'I'm not wrong. I feel it. Here.' She clenched her fist over her chest.

He shook his head, his mouth opening and closing. 'You shouldn't be feeling that at all.'

'But I am.' She took another step forward. He took a step back, hands held up as if to shield himself from her. 'I have never felt such horrifying loss before.' She blinked rapidly, tears welling in her eyes, choking on her words. 'I can't bear it. I don't know how you can. I don't know how you've managed to shield this from everyone. It's so —' her hand clenched again, hot tears poured down her cheeks, '— huge. So all-encompassing. How can you even think past it?'

He shook his head but didn't say a word.

She took another step forward. 'Please, Paul. Let me help. You can't deal with this alone.'

'I have to.' He turned away, hands wrapping around his body as if to hold himself together. 'There were consequences. Now I must pay them. There is no other choice.'

'There is always a choice.' She stepped up behind him, wrapped her arms around him again even though she had no idea what he was talking about. He stiffened and moved to pull away, but she held on tight. 'I know you don't like me, that you think I'm a pain, but I am the only one who has felt you hurting. And I can help. Let me take some of the pain.' Her wolf keened as she sent calm and warmth along the part of the Packbond that tied all the Were in Pack McVale to their coven. To Paul. The grabbing soul-clenching grief lessened slightly as she did so, and she took a big breath for the first time since she'd felt it, pushing more of her maternal healing down the bond. 'See, I can help,' she whispered.

'Ivy.' He turned in her arms, looking down at her. 'You shouldn't be so good to me.'

She smiled up at him. 'I know. You're an arse. I hate you.'

He laughed, although it ended in a sound almost like a sob. 'No, you don't understand. You shouldn't be able to do this, feel this. Why do you? Did I not do it right?'

She frowned up at him. 'What are you talking about?'

He was looking past her, out into the darkness. 'So sick. I was so worried. But tonight ... the zombie that woke up was gone. Alive, laughing, dancing. It wasn't wrong. I wasn't wrong. It was all as it should be. Finally.' His gaze came back to her. 'But why can you feel what you're feeling?'

She stared at him askance for a moment before saying, 'You know you're making absolutely no sense.' She gasped. 'You are having a vision. I know they cause you pain. Is that why you're so sad? Grieving?' Oh Goddess. For him to feel like this, the vision must be horrific. She loosened her hold on him. 'Is it about the pack? Is something terrible about to happen? Have you told Iris and our Alpha?'

'No. You're wrong. There's no vision. I've not had one for a month.'

He'd been holding onto the horror of this vision for a month? Something flickered in his eyes—even though there was only the moonlight, she could see it. 'But I can see the shadows of it. It's making your life miserable.'

'No. No, it's not. I fixed it. It won't happen anymore. It's done.'

'What's done? What did you see?'

He firmed his lips, shook his head and knocked her hand away. 'Whatever I saw, it's nothing to do with you.' Then he disappeared again leaving her gaping at empty space, his words winding around in her mind.

He was lying. She felt it in her soul. Her wolf was howling with the knowledge of it. Not only was he lying, but she knew suddenly without a doubt that he'd had a vision and whatever it was, it was about her.

But why would he care about what happened to her?

Her wolf whimpered and she wrapped her hands around her middle, suddenly chilled. Paul was gone and the horrifying sense of loss had retreated with him.

Except, it hadn't completely gone. An echo of it remained inside her.

An echo that didn't belong to Paul.

No.

That echo of grief was hers.

OVER THE NEXT WEEK, Ivy began to notice that Paul was avoiding her. More than was usual.

He didn't come with Iris for the weekly dinner at her home—usually he and Stellan delighted in teasing her and giving her shit, even though she was a wolf-grown. He didn't turn up at the pack meeting to discuss the vineyard and the farm and what to do with the milk from the dairy cows they'd bought last year. He didn't even turn up at the lessons she and the other maternal wolves took with Abby, Iris and him to learn more about the healing they could do as maternal wolves.

Nobody else commented on his absence though, so she could hardly ask. But it wasn't difficult to put two and two together.

He was avoiding her and it was because she'd pushed him and forced him into lying.

Lying about something to do with her. Something horrible.

She still couldn't get her head around him caring so deeply that it would make him feel so sad, so much pain. Or the fact that she seemed to be the only one who'd noticed anything was wrong. It made no sense.

She wished she could ask someone about it, but if she did that, then they'd go ask him and he'd deny it and then she'd look like the fool.

She needed more proof that he was lying. That he was holding something back from them.

Perhaps she should leave it alone. Was it really her job to find out what was wrong? He called her Poison Ivy and treated her horribly most of her life. She argued with herself about it over a few days, but each time the waves of grief hit her—which they were doing more and more—her argument fell apart and eventually, she gave in to the need to find a way to help. Besides, she had a feeling that the man she'd seen the night of Siobhan's mating ceremony, the one filled with so much grief and despair, was different from the Paul who'd been so awful to her—and not only because of the turmoil of emotions emanating from him. It was something else. Something deeper. Something that echoed inside her. And she could not let that go.

The next morning after this final resolution, she pulled herself out of bed—it was harder than it should have been, her energy levels still low—and during breakfast, asked Stellan what his plans were for the day. He was only on guard duty for Paul for the latter part of the day, but he did let slip that he was heading to the hot springs to meet up with Paul and a few other pack mates. Apparently, the witch from the McClune Pack was driving down from her King Lake compound to spend a couple of days here with a few friends and they thought going to the hot springs would be a good activity to do together.

'That's great. I'm glad they're getting to know each other.' She kept her smile in place even though that aching inside her throbbed, making her want to cry.

'Yeah. Although Paul doesn't seem to be as in to it as he was a week ago.'

'Really?'

'Yeah. I don't blame him, though. It must be super hard to have to deal with an arranged marriage.'

'Paul knows the pack would not expect him to accept someone he didn't like,' Callum McVale said as he sipped his coffee.

'He wants to do his duty, Dad,' Stellan said, piling more strawberry jam than was necessary—or healthy—on his toast. 'He knows how important it is for him to have children who follow in his footsteps and continue the Collins line. And we all know the best way of ensuring that is for him to handfast with a witch.'

'But Paul's happiness is important too. I hope he knows that.'

Stellan shrugged. 'I suppose so. We haven't really discussed it.'

'Perhaps you should,' Callum said, eyebrows lowered. 'That's what a true friend would do.'

Stellan's brows creased, his jaw squaring. 'I am a true friend.'

'Are you? Sometimes I think you and those other two reprobates we bound to him as guardians, don't take your role seriously. Paul is under a great deal of pressure. He needs friends more than guardians now. You are bonded to him. You should be there for him more than any others.'

'He's not talking at the moment, Dad.'

'Well you and Jackson and Luke need to find a way to make him talk. I can't say he seemed very happy at the mating celebration. He didn't dance or participate as he usually would. Not to mention he hasn't been participating in pack life.'

So, she wasn't the only one who'd noticed Paul wasn't acting normally. Although, she didn't think her father had noticed the depth of change that she had. But this was fascinating and went a long way towards backing up her determination to get to the bottom of it. For the health of the pack of course. She still couldn't stand Paul for himself.

As their father continued to lecture Stellan about his obligations as friend and guardian to their lone Pack Warlock, Ivy ate her break-fast and pretended not to listen, flipping through the newspaper.

'I get it, Dad. We'll try harder.'

'See that you do.' Callum swallowed down the last of his coffee and stood. 'I better get going. David is keen to create the new pinot, so if your mother asks when she gets back from helping Abby,' he said, looking at Ivy, 'Tell her I'll be gone all day.'

Ivy nodded. 'I'll leave her a note.'

Her father raised his brows. 'You're going out?'

She glanced at Stellan. 'I was kind of hoping to go to the springs with Stellan.' She rubbed her arms and rolled her shoulders. 'I'm feeling a bit achy and could do with a soak.'

Stellan's spoon hovered halfway to his mouth as his attention snapped to her, worry lining his face.

'Are you unwell?' Her father rounded the table to put his hand on her forehead.

Shit, she hadn't thought about their worry—she'd been too busy hatching her plan to get close to Paul and watch him. 'I'm fine,' she said, taking her father's hand in hers. 'I just sat at my desk too long yesterday trying to catch up with study. Don't be a worry-wart.'

Callum smiled wryly. 'That's my job, darling girl.' He bent and kissed her forehead. 'If you feel tired, remember to rest, okay? We don't want you overdoing things.'

'I won't.'

He pointed at Stellan. 'Help your sister clean up the dishes.'

'Of course,' Stellan said.

7

When their father had gone, Stellan angled her a look. 'You weren't bullshitting him, were you? You do look a bit pale.'

'Too much inside and not enough outside,' she said, waving her hand. 'Can I come with you today? A long hot soak sounds like heaven.' It did actually. She really was aching.

'Of course you can come if you're up to it. Do you need a massage now?'

She shook her head, hiding her smile. Since her illness, Stellan had been super nice and solicitous all the time—the big idiot did love her. 'Do you mind if I ask Siobhan and Chloe along as well?' Her friend would help her watch Paul and tell her if she thought he was acting strangely. Also, Chloe, being the Pack Librarian, was really good at finding out gossip. She would undoubtedly know some gossip Ivy hadn't heard while being laid-up.

'If you can get them out of their cottage, sure.'

He winked at her and she winked back. Then together they cleaned up the breakfast dishes and made plans to meet up in an hour down by the garage. The wolves could have run to the private hot springs that were on a nearby piece of land the pack had recently purchased, but Paul and the members from the McClune Coven wouldn't make the hike easily, so they would use a couple of the 4WDs to get there.

Ivy changed into bathers and grabbed a towel, then headed off to ask Siobhan and Chloe to come with her and word them up about watching Paul. She wouldn't tell them exactly why she was worried—her dad's concern had given her a legitimate reason to have them spy with her.

It took a lot of banging on Siobhan and Chloe's front door to get them to open up, but when they heard a trip to the hot springs was in the offing, they both agreed to come and raced around to get changed into bathers, throw on flowing matching kaftans—when had her friend had time to get all matchy-matchy with her mate?—and grab towels. As they walked to the garage, she filled them in on the conversation between Stellan and her dad. 'Have you heard anything?'

Siobhan looked at her askance. 'You're concerned about Paul? Since when did this happen?'

Ivy shrugged, trying to look nonchalant. 'Just because he's an arsehole much of the time doesn't mean I'm not concerned about him. He's pack. He's ours to look after. Also, he's the last of the Collins line.'

'That's true,' Chloe said. 'We all know what happens to a pack that doesn't look after its coven.'

Ivy leaned into Siobhan and whispered, 'Morghanna Cantrae's Curse.'

Siobhan shuddered dramatically and they both snickered.

Chloe frowned at her. 'It's not something to laugh over.'

Siobhan, instantly contrite, wrapped her arm around her mate's shoulder and kissed her cheek. 'I'm sorry, Chlo. We know how serious it is, but it doesn't help to be doom and gloom about it, does it?'

Chloe dipped her head. 'No. But you shouldn't make fun of the Curse either. It destroyed the entire McCrae pack five-hundred years ago. And if something happens to Paul before he can have offspring, we could trigger the Curse to enact on all the McVales.' She glanced over at Ivy. 'If there is something making Paul unhappy, it is our job to find out what and do something about it. It's good of you to want to help him, even though you don't get along,' she said to Ivy. 'And you can count on me. I will help you.'

'So will I,' Siobhan said, slinging her other arm over Ivy's shoulder. 'So, what's the plan of attack?'

Ivy shook her head. 'Just watch for now and listen to anything he does or says, or anything others say.'

'And if we hear anything that's worrying, we'll report it to Iris,' Chloe said.

'Sure,' Ivy said, even though, at this point, she'd rather Iris not be told because then Iris would want to interview her and she wasn't sure she could keep from their coven's leader the strange feeling Paul created within her—as if they were connected in some way.

Paul wasn't at the garage when they got there. Stellan was though, leaning against a wall and chatting with the three witches and one warlock who were standing beside a McClune Wineries 4WD.

'Hey, sis. Have you met Mariella?'

'No, I haven't. Hi, I'm Ivy.' The lovely diminutive witch who was set to marry Paul was like a pixie, all big eyes and heart-shaped face and wild-curling strawberry blonde hair, her dress swaying around her legs with every balletic movement as she moved forward, hand outstretched. Ivy felt suddenly big and clumsy.

Her wolf growled inside her as she shook hands with the witch. Mariella frowned—hell, had she heard that? Claws pricked under her skin and she snatched her hand away before she could hurt the witch with them. 'This is Siobhan and Chloe.' She gestured quickly at her friends.

Mariella greeted them. 'You had your mating ceremony last week I hear? Congratulations. May your love be eternal.'

Siobhan and Chloe each returned the traditional greeting of, 'And may you find your eternal love,' touching brow, lip and heart.

Mariella introduced her friends, Joseline, Frankie and Tony, and as they offered their congratulations to Siobhan and Chloe, Ivy took a moment to subdue the bitter sensation in her chest while watching Mariella closely. She had power—it rippled out from her, making Ivy's wolf hum inside and itch to get out—but she wasn't brash with it. In fact, if anything, she seemed kind of shy.

Siobhan—Goddess love her—punched Stellan in the arm and said, 'Hey, Drooler.'

Stellan rolled his eyes as the McClune visitors all smirked and Mariella asked, 'Drooler?'

He glared at Siobhan. 'Thanks, Ghoul.'

She grinned up at him. 'My pleasure. Always keen to warn others of your drooling problem.'

'I do not have a drooling problem.'

'Oh yeah. Steph says otherwise.'

He lifted his hands and made a squeezing motion with them as the McClune visitors snickered. 'You'll get yours,' he snarled.

Siobhan jumped behind Chloe and shook in mock fear, 'Oh no! Drooler's coming after me. Help, Chlo. Help.'

Ivy shook her head at them as the others laughed. 'Idiots.'

'I thought you'd grown out of baiting each other,' Chloe said, still chuckling.

'Never,' Stellan said.

'Too much fun.' Siobhan stopped cowering and slung her arm over Chloe's shoulder. She glanced around. 'Where's Paul and the others? I thought they were coming.'

Stellan dropped his hands and said, 'Paul's gone with Luke and Jackson to set up and do a temperature check of the different springs.'

'Why do they need to do that?' Frankie—a tall, dark-haired witch with startlingly blue eyes—asked.

He smiled down at her, his smile gentle—since when did her brother smile like that?

'The springs are all different temperatures and the temps can go up and down,' he explained gently.

'Is it dangerous?' Joseline asked, gripping Tony's arm.

'No. You won't get boiled or freeze,' Stellan assured her. 'But you just don't want to sit in one that's too hot for too long, so we do regular checks before we go in.'

'Oh, okay.'

'It sounds marvellous,' Mariella said. 'Should we get going?'

'I was just waiting for the baskets of food to get here—and here they are,' he said as Charlie and Max ran into the garage, holding two large picnic baskets, one each, and lugging a big esky between them.

Ivy went to grab a basket from Max to put it into the boot of the 4WD, but Stellan whisked it out of her hand. She would have snapped at him that she was capable of carrying a heavy basket a few paces to the car, but the big idiot was worried about her, so she just let it be and hopped into the 4WD with Chloe and Siobhan.

A few moments later, with Stellan in the McClune 4WD and Charlie and Max in theirs, they set off to the hot springs.

As they drove closer, Ivy's nerves sparked through her and she found it harder and harder to concentrate on the conversation going on around her. She plastered a smile to her face and tried to ignore the feeling growing inside her: dread.

But why dread?

Was it because she was afraid to find out what was wrong with Paul? She didn't think that was it. Her determination on that front hadn't wavered. Was she afraid to see Paul after that moment on the hill with him? She didn't think so. Nothing had happened. It wasn't like he'd seen into her soul or anything.

But as they drove closer to the springs, she struggled against leaping out and running as far away from the springs as she possibly could get.

Which made no sense at all. She was someone who faced things, especially when she'd made a determination to do so.

So why was the idea of seeing Paul now filling her with such dread?

It wasn't until they got to the springs and she tumbled out of the car that she realised that like the feeling of pain and grief she'd felt on the night of the mating ceremony, the feeling of dread wasn't hers.

As Paul came up to the cars to greet Mariella, the sense of dread deepened. He greeted her, smiling all the while, kissing the petite witch's cheek and helping her out of the car.

Ivy's wolf whimpered and a stab of something nasty and bitter drove through her.

Paul's head whipped up. His gaze met Ivy's.

For a brief moment, the overwhelming sense of dread was replaced by a piercing joy that made Ivy clutch at her chest, a little sound escaping her lips.

'Are you okay, Ivs?' Siobhan asked, her arm going around Ivy's shoulders as if to steady her.

'Fine,' she managed to get out as she returned Paul's gaze, unable to break it.

Mariella touched Paul's arm, drawing his attention back to her and the moment was broken.

She looked around. Had anyone else noticed? But everyone else was chatting and laughing as they headed up to the cabin that housed the change rooms. The only person who seemed the least concerned was Siobhan—and her concern was aimed at Ivy.

'I'm fine. I promise.' Siobhan's frown deepened into a 'don't shit me' look. 'The bumpy ride here just made me feel a little car sick, that's all,' Ivy lied. 'I just need some air.' She gestured up the hill where Paul and Mariella were almost at the cabin. 'Come on. We can't find out anything down here.'

Siobhan nodded, but kept her arm around Ivy as they went up the hill—bloody protective soldier. She really did love her friend, but she was being ridiculous. There was nothing to worry about. Whatever had made her sick had gone and she was fine. Just needed to build up her strength again, that was all.

But as she neared the cabin where Paul had disappeared inside with Mariella, that feeling of dread built again, and it was hard not to shake in the face of it.

She went into the female change room and quickly threw her clothes into a locker and wrapped a towel around her, hoping that Siobhan didn't notice her hands trembling or the tension that vibrated through her. Goddess, this feeling in her chest was awful. If it was Paul's, how the hell was he still walking and talking let alone smiling at his prospective partner. And why dread? That wasn't what she'd felt the night of the mating ceremony, or the echoes of what she'd felt since. And why was she still the only one feeling this?

She really needed to find out what the hell was going on because she didn't like this connection one bit.

As she rushed out of the change room, she smacked into someone coming out of the male changing room.

Warm, strong hands steadied her.

That joy pierced her again and she smiled up at him.

She looked up into vibrant blue eyes.

'Ivy.' Her name was whispered, a plea.

'Paul.'

His fingers tightened on her arms, his gaze dipping down to her lips. He swayed towards her—or did she sway towards him? Goddess, she wanted to feel his lips on hers. She'd never wanted anything so much.

Laughter sounded from behind her.

Paul let her go, blinking rapidly, the expression on his face tortured. 'Sorry. Sorry.'

'Sorry for what?' she asked, uncertain about what had just happened, or almost happened.

He shook his head, whispered harshly, 'You can't be here. Go. Please go.'

She didn't have a chance to respond as a voice from behind her said, 'Oh, you waited for me, Paul.'

He stepped around Ivy and held his hand out for Mariella. 'Of course. I wanted to make sure you and your friends had a bottle of water before we head up to the springs. You need to keep yourself hydrated.'

'I didn't bring one.'

'No problems. There's plenty in the car. Let's go get you one. Excuse me, Ivy.'

They moved around her and disappeared outside.

She stood there, breathing in and out deeply, trying to stop the racing of her heart and the feeling like she was about to throw up. Why had he asked her to go? Why tell her she couldn't be here?

Something was dreadfully wrong. Not just with Paul, but with her. And she needed to find out what before it drove her insane.

8

P aul couldn't believe his bad luck. He thought he'd been doing so well over the last week, avoiding her as much as he could. He'd never used his calming mantras so much, but they helped. He'd almost convinced himself he could live near her, that it would all be okay if he just kept his distance for a while.

Then he'd seen her step out of the car, so close, her beautiful eyes on him, and everything went to shit again.

She wasn't supposed to like him, so why was she seeking him out? And she was seeking him out. She'd looked for him the moment she'd got out of the car. And he'd heard that she'd asked after him at the various pack functions and meetings he'd avoided for fear of seeing her.

Hell. He thought having Mariella come down here to spend some time together would fix things. He did like the witch after all—she was kind and talented and very pretty, and she deserved some effort on his part to get to know her better, to allow her to get to know him better, before they made the decision that would bind them for life. But rather than create a distraction, for some reason, her presence seemed to be making everything so much worse.

He didn't want Mariella. The only woman he wanted—had ever

wanted—was standing beside the spring down the hill, her green one-piece hugging her curves in a way that made him shift uncomfortably where he sat. He had done everything he could throughout the morning to keep away from her. But every time he and Mariella moved to another spring, Ivy had soon followed. And despite the fact she was talking and laughing with the others in the group, he couldn't help but feel she was watching him. As was Siobhan and Chloe. They masked it well, not talking to him more than they did with the others in the group, but given he'd bound Ivy to a fate where she hated him and avoided him at all costs—which meant Siobhan treated him and his friends with dislike in support of her friend—it was strange that they were suddenly so keen to talk to him and be in his sphere as if they were friends.

Had she remembered something?

No. That wasn't possible. He'd done his job too well.

Then why the sudden and unnerving interest in him?

Her laughter lit the air with the brightness of the sun on a summer's day. She seemed to be enjoying herself—and yet, there was something wrong. He could feel it deep inside where the torn and aching threads of the mating bond were. She should be untouched by what he'd done because if she couldn't remember they were mates, then how could she be affected by the loss of it? Yet, she was weaker than she'd been. The light inside her dimmed. She put up a good front, but he could sense it. And he knew that if he looked, he'd see the effects of it on her aura.

Did Abby know? Iris? They must. They would have looked at her aura and seen that there was something wrong. Something missing.

She laughed again, and despite the bright joy in the sound, he heard an echo of sadness.

Had he caused that? Had he done something wrong when he'd changed their fate? Arianrhod had said there were consequences for messing with the Fates. He'd thought he would be the only one punished because he was the one who had cut and rewound the threads. Remembering Ivy as he did, the fact that they were mates, that she had loved him and that for a moment, she had been completely his, was the fiercest joy cut with the bitterness of deep welling grief. But he could deal with his suffering as long as she was untouched, as long as she was safe from the fate meant to be hers.

But he couldn't handle it if she was made to suffer too.

What had gone wrong? He had to figure it out and right it. Ivy deserved to live a happy life, not one tinged by some unknown sadness. He would have to look into her future—something he hated doing. Inviting the visions never made them easier to bear, so he rarely did it. But to protect Ivy, he would do anything.

'Paul?'

He jerked at the touch on his arm and turned to see Mariella looking at him. The frustration in her eyes told him she'd been trying to get his attention for a while. 'I'm sorry. My thoughts were wandering.'

'So I can see.' Her gaze flickered to Ivy then back to him. 'She's quite lovely.'

'Yes.' He wanted to call the word back as soon as he'd said it. 'I mean, I suppose she is. She's Stellan's little sister. I've never really looked at her that way.'

'Really?' The word was drawn out, full of nuance he didn't want to look at too hard.

'Yep. Umm, do you want to move to another spring? This one's quite warm and we shouldn't sit in it for too long.'

'Sure.'

She let him help her up and lead her to the cooler spring up the hill, just out of sight of where the others were congregated. He slipped into the water with a sigh, enjoying the slight effervescence of the mineralised water.

'This one's smellier than the others.'

'It's got minerals in it the others don't have. That's why it feels bubbly against your skin.'

'Interesting.'

Silence fell and he became super conscious of the fact they were truly alone for the first time since arriving. He should move to sit next to her. It would be the easiest thing to slip his arm behind her neck, to feel the side of her body flush up against his. He should want it.

He stayed where he was.

He should chat with her, ask her questions about her life, her training, her likes and dislikes.

He put his head back on the edge of the pool, closed his eyes and wished himself far away.

'Paul?' Her voice was a little sharp and he sat up with a jerk, eyes snapping open, searching around them for whatever threat had put that sound in her voice.

There was nothing. He looked back at her. Her gaze was pinned on his, eyes wide, her mouth opened a little to show the slight crookedness of her front teeth.

'What is it?'

'You started to fade.'

'What?'

She lifted her hand, droplets of water sparkles in the sun as she gestured at him. 'You were there and then ... you began to fade. I've never seen anything like it before. How did you do it?'

'What? What are you talking about?'

'It was almost like you were becoming a shade. But that isn't possible. You still have your soul.'

He stared at her, a little frisson of horror sparking to life inside him. 'It must have been a trick of the light. I didn't do anything.'

'I assure you, I was not seeing something. Ask her.' She gestured behind him.

He didn't need to turn to see who was there.

Ivy.

He didn't want to acknowledge that he'd felt her presence the moment she'd started up the hill, had been trying his utmost to ignore it, ignore the fact he knew she was coming closer, but now she was here, the impact on him was unavoidable. He held himself still, even though every part of him was longing to turn, to look at her, to breathe in the beauty of her spirit, the gentle energy of her wolf, the intensity of her blue eyes. His fingers tingled to touch; his lips longed for hers. Her scent—jasmine on a summer breeze—cut through the mineral smell of the water and teased his senses.

He wanted her.

He longed for her.

He could never have her.

'Ivy, tell me you saw what Paul just did.'

Ivy didn't come closer, but he felt her eyes on him as if she was standing right beside him, touching him.

'I'm not sure what I saw. It could have been the light.'

'It wasn't the light. Magic lit the air. You had to have felt it. Your wolf had to have sensed it.'

She didn't say anything but did come closer. She slipped into the water beside him, not close enough to touch, but close—too close. He shifted away. She made a small sound—of distress? Ah, shit. He didn't want to hurt her. His eyes went to her.

She was staring at him with that same look he'd seen in her eyes the night of the mating ceremony. As if she could see his pain. But that was impossible. He'd built so many barriers around his pain, impenetrable from even the most talented witch or warlock, there was no way she could sense it.

And yet, now, he was certain she could see his pain as if he was wearing it on his face. How?

He should go. He wanted to go.

He couldn't go.

But he must.

She gasped—as did Mariella.

'Paul.' Ivy reached out and touched him.

Her touch sparked through him, bringing life and light where there had been pain-driven numbness. He gasped.

'How did you do that?' Mariella's voice was a mere whisper.

He kept his focus on the witch, trying to ignore the fact Ivy still gripped his arm. Warmth shot out from that touch and it was so hard not to lean into it, wrap her in his arms and never let go. He swallowed hard. 'Do what?'

Mariella shook her head. 'Not you. Her.'

He looked then and instantly wished he hadn't. Ivy was staring at where her hand touched his arm, an expression on her face that was pleasure and pain combined. There was a slight glow emanating from where she touched him, remarkably like the glow a healer used when working their magic on a patient. But she wasn't a healer. She was a maternal wolf, her empathy really only tuned to pick up the needs of the pack as a whole, not the individuals in it. She did not have the powers of a pack healer.

And yet, there was that golden glow as she touched him.

He looked up at her face. Did she look paler than before?

A vision swam through his mind—Ivy on a bed, her face grey as death.

No. No, that couldn't be right. That was just his fear talking. He'd saved her. She wasn't going to die. That wasn't one of the ways he'd seen her die.

Another vision shot through him—Ivy staring up at him, her eyes full of tears and yet smiling, the lines around her eyes and mouth deeper, holding hints of wisdom. 'It's twins, my love.'

He jerked as it left him, nerves firing as if he'd had an electric shock.

'Paul.' Her voice brought him back.

Blinking, he looked down at where her hand still gripped his arm, the two visions of her overlaid with the reality of her. 'Ivy?' he asked slowly. He raised his head—it felt so heavy—to meet her gaze.

Her eyes were vibrantly electric as if lit by power within.

'What are you doing?' Mariella's voice was a slap, pushing the visions away.

'I'm not doing anything,' he said, unable to break Ivy's stare.

'Yes, you were,' Ivy whispered. 'You were fading and I touched you and you stopped.'

'Fading? I wasn't fading. I didn't do anything.' He managed to drag his gaze away, glancing at Mariella.

'You did something.' She tipped her head to the side, a deep furrow marking her brow. 'There was the strangest feeling of power. It buzzed around you and you began to fade again, just like a shade, but then she touched you and you stopped. Perhaps her healing powers stopped whatever it was from happening.'

'I am not a healer,' Ivy whispered, her voice husky.

'Then how?'

She looked up at the witch. 'I don't know. I shouldn't be able to do this.'

'And yet you are.'

The water lapped over them and the edges of the spring as Mariella stood and quickly made her way over to them. She held her hand over where Ivy touched Paul. 'You are right. This is not the kind of energy a healer uses. It's a bond energy.'

'The Packbond?' Paul asked.

She shook her head very slowly, her frown deepening as she closed her eyes. 'No. It's something else. Almost as if—' Her eyes snapped open and she stared at them.

'What?' Ivy asked as dread rose inside of Paul.

No. No. She couldn't know.

'What did you do?' Mariella asked him.

'Nothing,' he said too quickly.

'You've torn your soul,' she said as if he hadn't spoken. 'Why would you do such a thing?' She backed up a step, two, her eyes widening with horror.

'I didn't. I didn't do anything to my soul.'

Her hand rose, palm up, fingers splayed as if creating a barrier. 'I don't know why I didn't see it before, but whatever she's doing is allowing me to see it clearly.'

'What? Why? What am I doing?'

'You're healing the torn edges of his soul. I don't know how—it shouldn't be possible. Especially not for a maternal wolf with no powers. But I can't deny what I sense, what I see. His soul is torn and you are healing it.'

Ivy swallowed hard. 'Should I let go?'

'No!" Water surged around them as Mariella took a sudden step forward. 'Whatever you do, you can't let go. You are the only thing stopping him from turning into a shade.'

'I am not turning into a shade.'

'I know what I saw. She knows what she saw.' Her gaze returned to Ivy. 'You can't let go. If you do, we might lose him.'

'It doesn't matter,' she said, sounding a little drunk. 'I don't think I can let go.'

Paul snorted. 'Don't be ridiculous.' He really couldn't deal with sitting this close to Ivy any longer. It was torture. Especially as he could feel her in every pound of his heart, in every spark of every nerve. 'I need to go.'

'No!"

Mariella thrust out her hand and he was pinned to the spot. 'What the fuck? Let me go.'

Mariella shook, her nostrils flaring as if she was fighting tears. 'I'm sorry, Paul. But I can't let you break the contact with Ivy. She's the only thing keeping you here.'

'You are being overdramatic.'

'Am I? Look at yourself.'

He looked down.

At first all he saw was the glowing golden threads under and over his skin, emanating from the point of contact with Ivy. But then he noticed that under the golden threads, his skin held a grey sheen, like mist. And like mist, he could see through the areas where the golden threads had yet to reach.

Bloody hell. Mariella was right. He was fading. He was turning into a shade.

9

Ivy couldn't believe what was happening. How was it happening?

Paul had begun to fade again. It had terrified her and she'd grabbed his arm in panic and suddenly, he stopped fading. Now she couldn't let go. Something in her was feeding into him. Holding him here. Stopping him from becoming a shade. Whatever a shade was. She hadn't heard the term before but from the sound of Mariella's tone, it wasn't good.

Paul had stilled when he looked down, his shock rushing through her, punching the breath out of her lungs. He didn't want her to touch him. It hurt him. She wanted to let go, his desperation to get away from her slashing at her, hurting so deep it made her wolf whimper and howl.

But she couldn't let go.

What the hell was going on?

'I don't know,' Mariella said and Ivy realised she'd asked the question out loud. Or had Mariella heard her thoughts—she didn't know what the McClune witch's talents were. She hadn't listened as the group had chatted earlier, her attention too bound up with watching Paul, being aware of Paul. She had meant to watch him, but the way all her senses—wolf and human—focused on him was unnerving.

And now this. 'I don't feel very good,' she said as her head swam with the enormity of it.

'She's feeding me too much energy,' Paul said. 'Ivy, you have to let go.'

'No. She can't. If she does, I fear we'll lose you.'

'You don't know that. I can keep myself here.'

'You didn't even know you were fading.'

Ivy's gaze slammed from one to the other as they argued until finally, she broke through their voices and gasped, 'Get help.'

Mariella surged out of the spring and began to run down the hill, calling for help.

Water lapped around Ivy, the push of it battering at her, making her lose her contact with the wall—the only thing keeping her upright. She began to slide down as the waves caused by Mariella's departure faded. It was so warm. So gentle as it moved against her, around her. She could just sink down and down and—

'Ivy.'

Paul's arm slipped around her shoulders, pulling her up, holding her against him. Support. Comfort. She wanted it. Longed for it. She looked up at him, her vision swimming as if she was drunk. 'Thank you.'

'Don't thank me. I'm so sorry, Ivy.'

'Why are you sorry?'

'This is my fault.'

'What are you ... talking about?' Why was it so hard to get the words out?

'Hubris. I'm being punished for it. You're being punished for it.' He brushed damp hair off her forehead and cupped her face. 'I thought I was saving you. I thought I could change things.' He barked out a laugh. 'But Fate truly is a bitch.'

She reached up and touched his dear face—dear face? The thought surprised her but she couldn't deny the truth of it. She loved his face. 'Don't talk like ... that. The Fates ... will hear you.'

'Ivy.' He leaned down and pressed his lips to her forehead. 'It's way too late for that,' he said against her skin.

She wanted to ask what he meant, but her mind was such a muddle now and her lips suddenly refused to form words. She was sleepy. So sleepy. Her eyelids started to close.

'Ivy! Stay with me. Don't you leave me. You can't leave me.'

Her wolf whimpered inside her, clawing just under her skin as if wanting to get out, but somehow unable to manifest the change.

There was shouting, running feet. Water splashed around her, over her, lapping up to her chin,

'Ivy!"

Stellan? That was Stellan. Why did he sound so panicked? He was never panicked. He was a guardian. They were trained to keep their cool.

Why wasn't he keeping his cool?

'What's wrong? What happened?' More voices, more splashes, more water lapping over her. She coughed as some got in her mouth, the mineral taste buzzing under her tongue.

Paul's arms tightened around her.

'No, don't move her!" That was Mariella's cry, coming now from behind them.

'But she's sick. We have to get her back to Abby. She's probably having a relapse.'

Stellan's hands were on her, pulling, and then they were yanked away.

'Hey!"

There was growling all around—Luke and Jackson and maybe the other wolves who'd come today—so much violence in the air. And power. It sparked around her, shooting slivers of lightning across her skin, sinking into her pores. She moaned as the power sank into her, firing through her veins and down to her hand.

'Stop!' Paul's voice just above her head, his anguish screaming through her as his arms tightened around her. 'You're making her worse.'

'Ivy. Ivy.' Stellan sounded like he was fighting somebody—something—his voice strained. 'Let me take her to Abby. She's going to die if you don't let us go now.'

'Paul's going to die if you make her let go of him.'

'What?'

The word was shouted from multiple lips, violence a threat away.

'Why would you want him dead?' That was Luke. 'Is that why you came here? To kill our only Pack Warlock? Do the McClunes want war?'

'No. You misunderstand. She is the only thing keeping him here.'

'What are you talking about?'

'Look. Look at his skin. Look at where she's touching him. He's done something to damage his soul. He was turning into a shade—but she's keeping him here. Healing him.'

The water stilled around them as Stellan and the others stopped thrashing against whomever—or whatever—was holding them. 'What the holy fuck.'

She would have giggled if not for the fact she had no control over her body now, everything inside her pushing towards Paul. She could feel it so clearly now. She had no idea how or why, but there was an echo of a bond and she had linked to it, was channelling her wolf-energy into it.

Her wolf was giving itself up to save Paul. She was giving herself up to save Paul. To save the pack. He'd damaged his soul—was that what she'd been feeling?—and she, for whatever reason, was the only one who could fix it.

'What is she doing?'

'She's giving her lifeforce to save him.'

'How? She doesn't have the ability to do that. No wolf has the ability to do that.'

'They do if they're mates.'

PAUL JERKED AS IF PUNCHED. 'No. It's got nothing to do with that.'

'There is no true bond, you're right,' Tony said, eyes unfocused as he used his powers.

'But the tear in your soul is where a bond might be,' Mariella continued. 'There's one in her too. You said she was sick recently?'

'What did you do, Paul?' Stellan asked. 'What the hell did you do?'

He stared at his friend. What could he say? How could he explain? 'You don't understand. I did it to save her.'

'Does it look like you're saving her?' A menacing growl rumbled in his friend's chest. 'Are you the reason she was so sick? That she was in a coma? You were with her the night she fell ill. But I never thought ... How could you do this to her?'

'I didn't do it. I tried to save her. She was going to die. I couldn't let her die.'

'Enough!" Mariella snapped. 'We don't have time now for twenty questions. We have to get them back to Iris and Abby as quickly as possible. Maybe together we can stop her giving her lifeforce to save him.'

'How do we do that if we can't separate them?'

'Lift them carefully. Tony, Frankie and I will create a cushion of air around them as you lift. Josie, can you please monitor their auras? Let us know if there are any unexpected fluctuations.'

'I don't know what I'm looking for.'

'I think you will know if you see it. Now, on three. One, two, three.'

Paul wanted to help, but he was unable to move, unable to use his powers. Magic sparked around him and Ivy as the McClune Pack Witches wove a spell of air around them, a bubble of protection to make certain they weren't jolted as Stellan and cohort lifted them and carried them down the hill.

Ivy was semi-wound around him now, almost lying on top of him as they were carried, her arm lying across his chest where it grabbed his forearm. He curved his free arm around her back, gripping tight. Her free arm lay across his stomach, her fingertips grazing across his abdomen, the hard muscles under the firm skin twitching. Her head lolled on his shoulder, tucked under his chin.

It felt so right to have her there. But it was wrong. So wrong. He wanted to stop her from what she was doing, but didn't have a clue how.

It was too difficult to get them onto the back seat with the way they were 'attached', so they ended up in the boot of one of the 4WDs after Siobhan and Chloe had laid the back seats down flat. Stellan, Luke, Tony and Mariella crowded in with them to keep them from moving and to keep the bubble of cushioning air around them.

The car moved off over the bumpy dirt road. Ivy moaned as they were jolted.

Mariella said, 'We have to float them.'

'Okay.' Tony's voice sounded strained, but a moment later, they rose to float a few inches above the carpeting of the boot.

'Can you keep that up?' Paul asked them.

'We have to,' Mariella said, her voice as strained as Tony's had been. 'But you need to hurry,' she shouted over her shoulder at Jackson.

'I'm trying,' Jackson called back.

Ivy muttered something and Paul bent down to listen. '... in your arms. Warm ... right ... like way you smell.' Her head lolled on his shoulder and her eyes rolled up into her head.

He tightened his arms around her. 'Ivy. Ivy. Stay with me.'

'What's wrong?' Stellan said, voice panicked.

'She's falling unconscious. Can't you do something?' he asked Mariella.

'I don't know what to do.'

'You have to stop her from doing what she's doing.' His gaze searched for his friend's, begged.

Stellan reached for Ivy's hand, but Mariella stopped him. 'Don't.'

'But he looks more stable now.'

'That's only because of whatever she's doing. I have no idea what will happen if you take away the link between them. I haven't ever seen anything like this before.'

'But it's making Ivy weak,' Paul muttered.

Mariella's chin wobbled, her facial muscles twitching as if fighting back tears. 'I am sorry to say this, but she is one wolf in a pack of many. You are the one and only heir to the Collins line. I cannot stop her from doing whatever she's doing if it means you die. Not even if it means she will die.'

'No. She can't die. She was supposed to live.'

'What did you see, Paul? What did you do?' Stellan asked.

He shook his head, firmed his jaw. 'It doesn't matter. I can't take it back.'

'Stubborn warlock. Whatever you did is killing you.'

'That wasn't supposed to happen.'

'And you won't tell us what was supposed to happen?'

'No. At least, not to you. Not here.' His head bobbed a little, trying to make them see he couldn't discuss this in front of Ivy. Even if she was unconscious.

'Idiot.' The whispered word vibrated in his chest.

'Ivy?' Relief gushed through him, making him dizzy.

'You're awake.' Stellan leaned forward to touch her brow. 'What did you say, Ivy?'

'Idiot.'

There was silence and then a choked laugh. 'Is she calling me or you an idiot?'

'Paul,' she said. 'Although ... you too.'

Stellan choked out a laugh. 'Brat.'

She smiled then closed her eyes again. 'Sleepy,' she said.

'You need to keep your eyes open, Ivy, okay? I don't know what will happen if you lose consciousness.'

Ivy nodded. 'Hard.'

'Please, Ivy. For me.' He knew he shouldn't ask, but he was desperate.

'Okay,' she slurred, shifting her head to look up at him. 'Talk to me.'

He had no idea what he said—babbling nonsense—but he talked more than he'd talked for years.

'How long?' he heard Mariella whisper to Stellan.

'Ten minutes.'

Suddenly Ivy jerked, her eyes flaring wide.

'Ivy? What's wrong?

'My wolf? I can't feel my wolf.'

'What?' Paul said sharply. He looked up at Stellan, at Mariella and her coven mates. 'You have to do something. She can't lose her wolf. She won't survive.'

'I'm not bonded to your pack.'

'Please, do something.' A sob escaped him, tears wetting his face.

'I'll try.'

'Drive faster,' Stellan yelled.

The car jerked and bumped along the road, those in the back with him and Ivy doing their best to not bounce around while keeping as much energy on ensuring he and Ivy were in their stable bubble.

'We're here,' Jackson yelled soon after.

Car doors slammed and the boot opened and then they were moving again on their cloud of air. He was impressed that Mariella and Tony were still able to keep up the spell. They must be stronger than he'd realised. Then Abby and Iris were there hovering over them, shooting questions at everyone as they ushered them quickly inside.

They were taken into the loungeroom instead of an exam room and were laid on top of the table there. Mariella gave Iris and Abby a quick rundown about what she'd seen Paul then Ivy do and how they came to be here, her voice thick with exhaustion.

'That was quick thinking, girl,' Iris said. 'I thank you on behalf of Pack McVale for keeping a calm head. Sam's report of you is true.'

'Thank you. But I didn't do much of anything other than making sure they weren't separated. I just didn't know what was going to happen if they did.'

'From what you said, it was the right thing to do,' Abby said. 'But how was he fading? You mention a shade?'

'Yes.'

'You have to help Ivy,' Paul said, frustrated they were concentrating on what had happened to him and not the wolf in his arms.

Iris' worried gaze met his. 'I need to look at what you've done first. Abby, can you look at Ivy's wolf and see what's going on there?'

'Will do.'

'Link hands.' A circle of people surrounded them—Iris, Abby and the McClune witches and warlock—and then a strange humming sounded in the air as power sparked to life around them.

Ivy jerked in his arms a few minutes later, a growl in her throat.

'There you are, girl,' Abby said softly. 'Don't hide away. Come out and let me see what's happened to you.'

'Don't let her change,' Iris said.

'I won't. Just enough for me to see, gorgeous wolf. There.' Paul looked down to see Ivy's wolf in her eyes, the prick of her claws a welcome sting on his skin. Thank the Goddess. Thank the Goddess.

'What is this?' Abby said, eyes closed once more. 'It looks like—' She gasped, eyes snapping open. 'Do you see this, Iris?'

'I do.'

'How is this possible? When did this happen?'

'I don't know.'

'What happened?' Stellan asked.

But Iris shook her head. 'I need to speak to Paul and Ivy first. Thank you everyone for your help here, but Abby and I have this in hand. Jackson and Luke, please take Mariella and her friends to the hall and make sure they are fed and given a place to rest before they flame out. Stellan, perhaps you can go and get your parents. Ivy is going to need their support when we're finished. But tell them not to come in until we are done.'

Stellan nodded and ran out.

Mariella bent over the table, her fingers brushing his hair from his sweaty forehead, and looked him in the eye. 'I wish you well.'

'Mariella—' Paul began.

She shook her head. 'We can speak later. For now, you need to concentrate on doing what Iris and Abby say to fix what's been done.'

He stiffened. 'That's impossible.'

'You have to try.' Her fingers stilled on his forehead. 'So much pain. So much guilt. I wish I was the one who could heal you, but—' her eyes flickered to Ivy, '—I don't think that is destined to be my role in this world.' She sighed, smiled sadly and then left with the others.

'Fuck,' Paul said.

'Language,' Iris remonstrated. 'Now, let me see if I can alleviate this power drain and then we will talk.'

Paul's arms tightened around Ivy as she made a whimpering sound. 'Stay with me, Ivy.'

'This might hurt,' Iris said.

Ivy screamed.

10

'Can you pull back a bit, Ivy?'

She blinked her eyes open at the question. She'd floated away after Iris had poked at the broken thing inside her, the pain an echo she could still feel. 'What?'

'Try and pull back the power you're feeding into Paul.' Iris's face wavered over her as her eyes focused.

'How?' She didn't even know how she was doing it, so how could she change how she was doing it?

'Close your eyes and think about pulling back.'

'But what about Paul?'

'We've got him. He won't fade away just yet.'

'Yet?'

'We're still not sure what he's done, but we've got him for now. You can pull back.'

'For now?' She shook her head, thoughts suddenly much clearer. 'If whatever you're doing isn't a long-term solution, then I'm not going to stop. I'm not putting Paul in danger.'

'You have to.' Paul's voice vibrated through her head—she was still lying against his chest. She should feel embarrassed, but she didn't. It felt too right.

'No. You can't make me do something that will hurt you.'

'Ivy, please. For me. Save yourself. You have to save yourself.'

She moved her head to look up at him—whatever Abby and Iris were doing had made her feel better. He looked better too despite the direness of their uncertainty. 'We can't lose you,' she said. *She* couldn't lose him. Her wolf couldn't lose him.

'It is very honourable of you, Ivy,' Iris said. 'But the danger isn't as great as it was when you were brought in and you can't continue to feed your life energy into Paul. The pack needs you too.'

'Why? I'm not anything special. There are dozens of maternal wolves more special than me. The pack does need Paul, though, if it is to survive.'

Paul began to push at her. 'No. You have to stop.'

'Paul. Cease struggling,' Iris hissed. 'You're making this more difficult.'

'But you have to make her stop it, Aunty. I can't lose Ivy.'

'You already have, you stupid boy,' Iris snapped. 'You cut the mating bond.'

Ivy stilled, the words ringing in her ears. Mating bond? But that couldn't be. They weren't mated. And yet ... Images flickered in her head of kissing him and touching him and there being so much joy it filled her soul.

'This wasn't supposed to happen.' Paul's words brought her back with a snap. 'She was supposed to be fine. She wasn't supposed to remember. I changed it.'

A chasm opened up inside her, one dark and deep and filled with pain. He'd rejected her. Somehow, they'd mated but he'd rejected it. Her wolf howled and she couldn't help but let out a sob. 'You don't want me.' She wanted to pull away from him, crawl into a dark corner and die. Would have if she could have.

'No. Don't go, Ivy.' Paul's voice was a rough whisper. 'You don't understand.'

Deep inside she felt him wrap around her and her wolf, hugging, holding tight, not letting them slip away.

'Paul. Stop that. Abby, can you pull her back?'

'I'm trying, but she's so hurt. I don't know why I didn't see this before.'

'Because my stupid nephew has played with fate. None of us could have seen what he'd done until Ivy started to remember.'

Remember?

An image fluttered in her mind—of Paul pulling her to him, his lips on hers, his fingers digging into her hair, his need filling her as something fell into place deep inside her.

Then he'd stilled, tensed, his fingers digging into her flesh. She pulled back. His eyes were black and there was a look of such terror and despair on his face. 'No,' he said. 'No.' Then he pushed her away.

Goddess. It hurt. His rejection had hurt so much. She'd tried to stop him, but she couldn't move. Then there was a tearing, a horrible tearing, and the world turned in on itself and she was hurtling through the void.

'Ivy, hold on. I've got you.' Abby's scent was inside her, her warmth wrapping around both her and her wolf. She leaned into the soothing warmth that was the healer, but it didn't help. It didn't help. She was broken. There was no recovering from the tear inside. How had she not felt this before now?

But she had. She had. The echo of it in her had recognised the echo of it in him. It's why she'd felt his pain and nobody else had.

A mating bond had sprung into place between her and Paul and he'd rejected her. Rightly so. Because the pack needed him to hand-fast with Mariella. The pack needed the witch to start a new, stronger generation with him. They needed her powers. Her strength. They didn't need a maternal wolf with no special powers except for an affinity with children.

He'd rejected her to save the pack. And to save the pack, she was willing to give herself.

'It's okay. It's okay,' she said, her voice trembling past the pain. 'Let me save you.' She closed her eyes and concentrated on the flow of energy that was going from her to him. It had been slowed by what-ever Iris and Abby were doing, but she couldn't let that continue.

They didn't know how to fix what Paul had done. She could hear it in their voices.

Only she could save him, with her full lifeforce.

Her death would be a sadness for her family and friends but they would all be safe from Morghanna Cantrae's Curse and that was all that mattered. That and the fact Paul just couldn't die. She couldn't bear the thought of it.

She turned her head to look up at him. 'Let me save you,' she repeated pushing past the magical filter Abby and Iris had used to slow down the flow of her lifeforce into him. Now she knew what she was doing, what was at stake, it was nothing to break the barrier and keep doing what she'd started at the hot springs. A thing she was capable of because he was her soul mate. He might have changed their fate, broken the bond in this thread of time, but they weren't simply mate-bonded. Their souls were bound through time and space. He could not tear that bond, no matter how much he tried.

It was there, a fine thread inside her. One she could use to save him.

'Ivy, no.' Paul's cry was in her ear, in her mind. He started pushing against what she was doing, his own energies flooding into her.

'Paul. Stop.'

Iris's voice was a distant echo to the same desperate cry deep inside Ivy. Her desperation allowed her to push up, to stare into Paul's eyes again. 'Please. Let me do this. I'm not important.'

He cupped her face with his free hand. 'You are to me. You must live.'

She shook her head. 'Not if it means you will die.'

'I will die without you.'

'No. You won't. We are not mates.'

'But we are. We are.'

She shook her head sadly. 'You didn't let it happen.'

'You remember?'

She blinked against the tears pressing against her eyes. 'You kissed me. Then you pushed me away. And I ... it felt like dying.'

'No.' His fingers clenched in her hair, his thumb brushing over her cheek. 'You weren't supposed to remember.'

'I didn't. Not until I touched you.' Her tears wet his bare chest, but she couldn't make them stop. 'I understand that you don't want me. That you can't want me. I'm not the right one for you at this time. You must do what's right for the pack. I understand.'

'No, that's not—'

'Let me go, Paul. Let me save you and then go and bond with Mariella. I give you my blessing. For the well-being of the pack.'

She took a breath and concentrated, pushing everything she was into him. She felt him scrabbling against her, trying to push back what she was giving him, but she wouldn't let him. She didn't matter. Only he did for now. They would get their chance again in some other life.

In this one though, this was the only thing, the one last thing she could do for the man who was meant to be her mate. It was all she could do for this man she'd loved all her life.

Save him.

Save the pack.

It was as simple as that.

She closed her eyes and gave him her life.

'Ivy, no!" Paul pushed against the power flowing into him, but it didn't help. She'd already gone limp at his side. His gaze met his aunt's. 'Please. Don't let her do this.'

'I don't know how we can stop her.'

'You have to. I can't live without her.'

'We can't live without you.'

'Then fix this.'

Iris glanced at Abby who shook her head, tears in her eyes. 'There's nothing I can do,' the wolf-healer said.

'Aunt. Please.'

'I don't know if I can.'

'Please. Try.'

Iris's jaw clenched as she pressed her lips together and touched Ivy. She gasped and grabbed her hand back a moment later. 'Abby, they're soul-bound.'

Abby's mouth dropped open as her gaze ran over Ivy. 'I had no idea. I never felt in her the return of an old soul.'

'That's because I don't think she is an old soul. Neither is he. They're brand new.'

'Then how can they be soul-bound?'

'I don't know. But look. You'll see it's true.'

Abby touched them both on their chests, her eyes closing for long seconds—too long. Ivy's lifeforce was flowing into him too fast.

Then the healer's eyes snapped open on her gasp. 'It's true. Do you think—?'

Iris nodded. 'Yes. It's the only way.'

'What are you talking about?' Paul demanded. He'd learned nothing of this in his studies.

'No time to explain now,' Iris said. 'But if it is true, we might be able to undo what you've done.'

Paul grabbed her wrist before she could lay a hand on him. 'No. If you undo it, she will die.'

'How can you be certain?'

'I saw it.'

'You better than anyone knows the future can be changed.'

'Not this one. It is a static point. If she mates with me, she will die.'

'And if we don't undo what you've done, you will both die. Ivy in the next hour and you soon after because she is the only thing keeping you here.'

'There has to be a way around it.'

'There isn't.' Iris's eyes bored into his, hard as flint, but with a touch of empathy at their depth. 'Either way, she will die. It is up to you when and how.'

Paul gritted his jaw until he thought his teeth might break. 'Then let me die with her now. I can't live without her.'

Iris' eyes flared with anger and determination. 'That is never going to happen.' She tore her wrist out of his grip as Abby put a hand on Paul's chest and one on Ivy's head at the same time that Iris laid her hand on his head and one over Ivy's chest. He tried to move, to slap their hands away, but the moment Iris touched him, it was like the world around him thickened.

'No. No. What are you doing? I don't want this,' he managed to say before his jaw locked and he could do nothing more than shout in his mind.

Iris's stern gaze met Abby's over the two prone bodies. 'Now.'

There was a sharp buzz in the air over him and then a terrible sting at the point Ivy's hand clung to his arm. The stinging turned to a burn, then a flame that raced through him. He cried out in his mind, could hear Ivy screaming in hers.

Iris and Abby—they were somehow inside him, inside Ivy, taking the filaments of broken bond and binding them together with filaments of something silvery and gold and glowing.

The soul-bond. The reason his try at changing fate and breaking the mating bond hadn't worked. He and Ivy were soul-bonded. A bond that stretched beyond life, beyond death. One that made them mates for all time. It was rare. So rare he'd never considered the possibility it could ever be his.

But if they used the soul-bond to rebuild the mating bond, wouldn't that tie their souls into this life?

And what happened in this life would be repeated through the soul-bond down through the ages.

Ivy would die over and over because she mated with him.

No. No! He couldn't let them do it. But he had no ability to stop them as they bound his and Ivy's souls into the mating bond of *this* life. He had no healing powers, nothing offensive with which to stop them, to shove them away. 'Goddess, Arianrhod,' he called in his mind. 'Please, help me now.'

A gaping void of sound was his answer.

He tried calling out again. Still nothing. Why didn't she come? She'd always come when he'd called in the past. Now, there was nothing. Arianrhod was gone and he was on his own. Another consequence of his actions?

It didn't matter. The beat of Ivy's heart next to his was getting stronger—a song in his heart—but he knew, if he allowed this, one day soon it would stop for good.

He wrapped all the power he still had inside him, knowing what he must do. The pack would find a way to survive without him. They still had Iris. She *could* bond other witches and warlocks to the pack. She'd find a way to make other covens and their packs agree.

She had to.

Ivy had to survive.

He folded space, sliced an opening into the void, and tore himself away.

11

Relief rushed through Paul as he transported himself away—he'd saved her! It lasted all of one second before he realised Ivy had come with him. Her hand was still clamped to his arm, her heartbeat a driving force next to his, her lifeforce feeding into him as she stared up at him with her big beautiful eyes.

The drain of lifeforce was slower now, the need for it not as great as it had been because of what Iris and Abby had managed to do before he transported himself away.

But she was still giving her life for his.

He had to stop her, but he couldn't remove her hand from his arm in the void. If he did, she would truly be lost.

Why? Why?

Why didn't Fate want her to live?

The void shifted and changed, the intent of his transportation spell moving them back into the real world with a thrust he was unaccustomed to.

They were thrown through the fold he'd created and landed with a hard thud, rolling through the long grass on top of the hill. He wrapped his arms around Ivy, protecting her as much as he could from their violent landing.

They came to an abrupt halt against a tree.

A tree? There shouldn't be a tree here. Had he miscalculated?

Not that it mattered. All that mattered was Ivy and what it meant that she'd come with him.

He lifted off her, trying to pull away, but her hand was still attached to his arm with that strange golden force that had sprung to life at the hot springs. 'Ivy, why did you do it? Why did you come with me?'

She looked up at him, her beautiful eyes achingly certain. 'I thought you were meant for Mariella. I was ready to sacrifice myself for that belief. But when Iris and Abby started to do what they did, I realised I was wrong. I couldn't let you go. You're mine to protect.'

'But I was trying to protect you. To save your life.'

She scrambled up to kneel beside him, the way she was attached making her brush up against him, sending shivers of longing through him. 'By forfeiting your own? You should know that cannot be allowed.'

'I cannot have you die because of me!"

She jerked back a little, eyes widened as his shout echoed around them. Then frowning, she said, 'You mentioned visions? Of me dying?'

'Yes,' he hissed. 'As we were mating I saw it. So many times through so many different threads. I tried and tried to see if I could change it, but nothing worked. Every future showed the same thing— if we mated, you would die.'

'Show me.'

He reared back, scrambling to his feet, but of course, she came with him, her fingers tightening on his arm. 'I can't do that.'

'Why not? Why are you the only one allowed to see what happens in our future?'

'My gift is given to me. The burden mine alone to carry.'

She stepped closer to him, touched his face. 'What law says that is so?'

'What?'

'There is no law that states you must shoulder the burden of your visions alone. No law that states you alone must change them and watch if you fail thinking it is entirely your fault.'

'But that is the way it has always been. I see the future and it is my job to find a way to stop the disasters from coming.'

'But don't you share your visions with the pack's leaders?'

'When it's something they can help me change.'

She smiled at him. 'Then you can share your visions.'

'What? No. That is not what I meant. Even if I tell them about what I see, I am the one who mostly decides what must be done because nobody but me can go into the visions to figure out the different paths to take.'

'But what if it doesn't have to be that way? What if you don't have to be the only one to decide what must be done?'

'It isn't possible. For that to occur, you would have to come into the vision with me, and I don't know any seer who has ever been able to make that occur. The visions are for the seer alone to bear.'

He'd stepped away as he spoke, but she came with him, moving even closer until he could feel the warmth of her along his front, her breath on his skin.

'But what if it can be done?' She reached up and touched his face, her fingers sliding down from his brow to his chin.

He knew he should refuse her touch, but in this moment, he couldn't make himself step away. Her touch was pleasure and agony combined. His heart throbbed with its need for the contact. He swallowed hard, forcing himself to not reach for her. 'It can't.'

'I think it can.'

'You're wrong.'

'Am I? You brought me through the void to this place. Why not take me into your vision?'

'That was simply a transportation. A mistake. It isn't the same.'

'Have you done that before? Transported someone with you?'

'No. It's not something that can be done.'

'Then how did you do it now?'

His mouth opened with a reply, but there was none. She was

right. He had been taught he could only transport himself, but he had just proved that teaching wrong. 'It's different,' he said weakly.

'I think it's the same. If you wanted to, I know you could do it.' She stumbled a little.

'Ivy.' He grabbed her arms, pulling her closer to steady her. 'Why are you doing this? You need to let go of me. You need to leave this place. If you don't, you won't survive.'

She looked up at him. 'If you want to save me, you need to mate with me.'

'If I do that, you will die.'

She shook her head, a little chuckle erupting from her mouth. 'This is a circular argument. I will die now if you don't mate with me and I will die if I do mate with you.'

'You could live if you would just let go.'

'Then you would die. And I would die with you.'

'No.'

She cupped his face, her thumb rubbing over his cheek. 'You may have broken and changed the threads of our mating, but they are still there, deep inside because we are soul-bonded. It's what is allowing me to give you my life energy to save you. It's what allowed Iris and Abby to start weaving those threads back together. Fate may have allowed you to cut the mating bond of this life, but it didn't allow you to get rid of the soul-bond. I am your fated mate. Not just in this life, but through time.'

'How can I live knowing our mating will be responsible for your death?'

'You take too much on yourself. It's no wonder you are always so unhappy.' She frowned, rubbed her head. 'I have two memories of you in two different life threads vying for pre-eminence in my mind. In both of them, you are so unhappy. It makes my soul ache to see it so.'

'You shouldn't be able to remember the other timeline.'

'But I can. Maybe it is this place.'

'What? My hill?'

'This isn't your hill, Paul.'

He lifted his head and truly looked around for the first time. It was his hill, but it looked different. There was a vividness to the colours of the grass and trees and sky that wasn't usual, like he was seeing everything through a golden tint.

It wasn't just the colours that were different. The grass wasn't quite right. It was blowing in a breeze that wasn't there and the clouds hung in the sky, unmoving, as if painted in the violet sky. Scents hung in the air that did not belong on his hill—cinnamon and honey and spicy scents mixed with the scent of exotic blossoms on the tree overhead.

A tree that shouldn't be there.

A tree as ancient and gnarled as any tree he'd ever seen, with a crown of gold and amber leaves arching over them. The leaves shivered on its branches, emitting a bell-like sound he'd not noticed until now because he'd been so focused on Ivy and trying to get her to leave him. But now he did notice it, he realised he'd heard that sound before.

This was the Goddess's place between time. The place she drew him to whenever he'd called to her for guidance, comfort and help. He'd never seen his hill here, strange tree or no, but he knew this was her place. The magic of it, the timelessness, sparkled on the air around him, tingling his skin, filling him with an energy he never felt at any other time.

'Arianrhod?' A breeze caught his hair, brushed over his skin. 'My Goddess? Why have you brought me here?' She did not answer as she usually did. Nor did she appear. 'What do you want of me? What point are you making?'

Only the bell-like chiming on the tree answered him, a word whispered to him in their sound: Choose.

'Choose? Choose what?'

IVY STARED up at Paul as he shouted at the sky, at the tree. She looked around. 'This is the Goddess's place?' A shiver trembled over her skin, but then a voice whispered in her ear, 'Help him. Help carry the burden. Help him to choose.'

'Choose? Choose what?'

She said the words at the same time he did. Their gazes met as their words echoed into the distance. She saw the world in his eyes—past, future, present, different time lines, different threads. The burden of knowledge so great. So heavy. And one she knew she could help to carry if only he would let her.

She had to convince him to let her. But to do that, she had to see what he could see.

A thought pressed into her mind, a whisper of knowledge, telling her how it could be done. She could dive in, using the threads of what bound them together and see what he saw. But she didn't want to force him to share. She wanted it to be his choice.

'Paul.'

He started to shake his head, his dark curls flopping over his fore-head in that way she so loved—even in the timeline where she'd hated him, she had still found the way his curls flopped on his fore-head like that annoyingly cute. She brushed the curls back, the silk of them warm on her fingers. He stilled under her touch. 'Paul.'

'No, Ivy. Don't ask me to do it.'

'You do not know what I want to ask.'

'Yes, I do. You want me to show you all futures I saw in which you die. But how can you ask me to do that to you? It was hard enough to see it without you viewing it with me. Why would you want to see it?'

Her mouth dried. She'd not thought of it like that—watching herself die over and over was something she didn't really want to see, but if it was inevitable ... 'Because there's a choice we can make.'

He sucked in a breath. 'What do you mean?'

'If my death is inevitable—whether we mate or not—then we should choose together which way it should unfold.'

'We? But I am the seer and—'

'Yes, we. Because we are mates—you cannot deny it—and a future that affects one of us affects us both.' She gripped his hand, brought it up to her chest, placing it there to feel her heart, then put her hand over his heart. 'See, they already beat as one. So let's act as one. You already tried it by yourself and look how that turned out.'

'I did what I thought was best.'

The hurt in his voice made her smile softly. 'I know you did, my mate. But it was the wrong choice to try to deal with this alone. Can't you see that? You have been given a mate—against the wishes of the pack and the coven and maybe history itself, we have been fated to be together. So let's be together. Truly together. In every decision. In every burden. Let's do what others only speak about and truly become one.'

'But ...' His voice faltered, his hand clenching against her chest. 'How can you want to see yourself die? To choose the manner of your death.'

'I don't. It fills me with horror to think of knowing when and how I will die.'

'Then how can you consider asking me to do this? How will you bear it?'

'Because, I don't think of it as choosing a death. I think of it as choosing a life.'

He stared at her. 'You are so strong. I wish I was strong enough to see it the way you do.'

She cupped his face again. 'Of course you are strong. How can you not see it?'

'The visions—they make me weak. I scream and cry and sometimes even pass out when having them. How can you call that strong?'

'Because despite what they do to you, you keep going back in. Keep opening yourself up to them to help others.' She placed her finger against his lips when he went to argue. 'I know you can block them. I've heard Iris and Abby talking about your stubborn refusal to let them help you keep them at bay to give you some respite and peace. But you never did. You kept having them for the good of the pack. If that is not strength, then what is?'

His mouth opened, closed, opened again. 'It is what I have to do.'

'But not alone. Not anymore. Never again. I am your mate. I never truly knew what that meant until now.' She'd always thought herself a little useless to the pack, not having a skill or role that was truly unique or added in some significant way to make the pack stronger. But she realised now that she was unique. Her dogged determination to just keep going and do her best, to see the bright side of things, was her strength. It was a quiet strength, but one none-the-less. One that added something essential to the pack.

And now, that quiet strength in her was the very thing finding a way forward for her and Paul. She could see it working on him, the bleakness leaving his eyes to be replaced with something that could be hope. 'Let me share this burden with you, starting now.' She took his hand in hers and held it up before them. 'As one, let us decide which fate shall befall us. Let us choose which path our lives should unfold. If we are fated to die as mates, then let us seek out the path that gives us the most time, the most happiness before the inevitable falls on us. Pushing the future aside, trying to change it, has made things worse. Let's not do that anymore. Let's embrace what is before us—our mating and the joy that will bring. Let this be our rebellion.'

'Our rebellion?'

'Yes. Our rebellion. To not only take what is offered and make the most of it, but choose the path that will give us the most. What do you say? Shall we tell Fate, "Fuck your ideals of control" and be the masters of how ours unfolds?'

His smile was a wide slash on his face, shining from his eyes as he lifted his hands to cup her face. 'I never thought I could love you more, but I do now. I think our love will keep growing.'

'Forever.'

'Yes, forever.'

His smile slipped a little. 'But Iris and Abby—they started to tie the soul-bond into this life's mating bond. If we do this, our fates will be inextricably linked to a tragic end.'

'Not if we don't wish it to be. I think we can find a way.'

'How? We won't remember what has happened in this life.'

He was right. There was no way to circumvent the fact that because of what Iris and Abby had started, their future lives would be bound down the same path they took on this one. They would find each other in every life their souls were granted, they would mate and then they would die.

The tree. The leaves. Memories.

The voice whispered in her mind and she reached up and touched the leaf hanging above their heads. At the touch, images flickered through her mind, showing them landing in the field to roll to a stop under the tree. It flickered forward, like a movie jumping ahead, showing them standing there in this spot, having this discussion. She gasped. 'The leaves. This tree. It will remember for us. And one day, we will discover it and we will know. We will remember and the memories will help us to right what has been wronged.'

He reached up and touched the leaf, gasped. Then touched another, eyes widening. 'They are my memories.'

As this is your place, the breeze murmured so that both of them heard. *Yours and Ivy's. Forever.*

'The Goddess is helping us,' Ivy whispered.

'I thought she'd forsaken me.'

Never. I am with you both, always, the voice said in the chimes of the leaves that rustled over their heads.

Paul stared down at her. 'This is because of you.'

'It is because of both of us. Now, let us fix what has been broken and decide our future, together.'

12

Paul gripped both her hands then gasped, holding them up to look at them. She'd let go of him, was no longer feeding her life force into him. When had she done that?

Not that it mattered. He was no longer going to send her back so that he could die alone. He knew now that was the wrong path. She'd helped him to see the truth of that.

She'd also helped him to see that he didn't need to do this alone.

The burden had never been his to carry because she wasn't the only one who died. They both did. Every time. He'd just been so focused on her death, he hadn't taken any notice of his. This fate, it wasn't her fate alone.

It was theirs.

He nodded. 'How do we do this?'

'You know,' she said.

And he did.

He bent his head and kissed her, starting the magic of a mating all over again, undoing all he'd done, pouring himself into it, heart and soul.

She met the kiss with equal passion opening to him and giving herself over to the bliss that was this touching, this melding, this oneness.

He broke the kiss and pulled back to look into her eyes. Full of love and trust and belief in him, his ability, his strength. He'd not allowed himself to see it before—had always thought his feelings were one-sided because he'd seen himself as weak. What an idiot he'd been. She'd been there all along, ready to share, ready to buoy his strength. He'd wilfully ignored her and then wilfully tried to change what had always been meant to be because he couldn't handle what was ahead of him. Ahead of them.

But she had been ready to handle it. And with her at his side, he knew now he was more than strong enough to face anything that lay ahead of them. Including choosing their life's path.

Like her, he refused to think it was about their deaths.

He stroked his fingers into her chestnut mane, the red in its depths echoing the fire of passion raging inside him. Her eyes were alight with it too, and clear, so clear and pure. It was all he could do to stop himself from joining with her now. But they couldn't give in to the wild urge yet. If they wanted to choose the path ahead, then they must do that first before sealing their bond and their fate.

She smiled up at him and even though he knew the brutality of what was to come, he smiled back. How could he not bask in the sun that was her?

'I love you, Ivy.'

'I love you too, Paul. Even in the false timeline you created that made me hate you, I loved you. I couldn't stop.'

'I'm sorry I did that to you.'

She stroked her hands through his hair then cupped his face. 'I'm not. What you did brought us here and now we can do this together.'

He cupped her face and stared into her eyes. 'Ready?'

'Always.'

'Close your eyes and reach down deep inside to the silver and gold threads.' He didn't have to tell her though—she already knew. Of course she knew. She could have done this without him. She already had access to the place his visions came from because they were soul-bound. She didn't need her own magic because she had his. But she hadn't done it without him, hadn't chosen for him. She'd given him the choice to choose this path. Just as he should have always given her one. He'd been such an idiot. But no more.

He leaned his forehead against hers, closed his eyes and sank inside.

She was there, waiting for him in the void, staring at a swirling pool of fog lit up by lightning flashes within. She turned, held out her hand. 'Show me,' she said.

He gripped her hand, tight, pulling her to his side. Then he opened his vision-sight and showed her all the paths that lay ahead of them once they mated.

The boat. The car. The kitchen where they got electrocuted, the field where he got stung and died of anaphylactic shock.

They died, over and over—more car accidents, boat accidents, hiking accidents, strange illnesses.

She stiffened at his side as she watched the litany of horrible futures that was theirs to choose from, but she didn't once look away. Didn't once cry out or shed a tear. Just asked him to stop the visions at times so they could poke and prod at the sides of them to figure out the cause—but the cause could never be changed, as he'd said—and to look at the path that led them there, how long that timeline gave them.

He expected to be overwhelmed by the desperation, the hopelessness he'd experienced the first time he'd seen these futures, but it didn't come. Her hope buoyed him as they looked for the future that gave them the most time, that gifted them the most happiness.

'Stop,' she said. 'That one.'

Paul stared at the image before them, backed it up, let it run forward, the expression in his eyes reflecting the horror of their final moments in this future.

IVY SWALLOWED HARD. It was probably the most violent of visions that she'd seen, almost like something out of a movie.

'This one's new. I didn't see it before,' he said after a moment, his tone wondering.

'Are you sure?'

He nodded. 'I would remember seeing this.'

She looked back at it. 'Maybe it's become a possibility because we've changed something.'

'Maybe.'

She watched as he let it play over again.

They were driving along a darkened road, the moon hiding to peep out occasionally through the clouds. They both looked worried, stressed, older. Much older. There were white strands in the auburn threads of hair at Paul's temple and lines around her eyes and mouth that weren't there now.

Vision-Ivy reached for vision-Paul's hand. As they touched, heat sparked out, the world span and Ivy was pulled into the scene …

Paul squeezed her fingers, his eyes meeting hers for a brief moment. 'It is time,' she heard in her head.

'Yes,' she answered back.

He lifted her hand, kissed her knuckles before letting go to return both hands to the steering wheel. There was danger sparking on the air and despite the fact they needed to touch to help keep them calm, it was more important for him to keep his wits about him.

The children had to survive this night. It was imperative.

Ivy glanced into the back seat. At her beautiful twins. She still couldn't believe they were hers. She felt luckier than she'd ever thought possible.

She smiled softly at them, trying to hide her desperate sadness over what was about to happen. 'How you going, Skye?'

'Fine, Mummy.'

'And you, River?'

'I'm good.'

'Remember what we talked about? The promise you made?' Paul said. She glanced back at him to see his fingers tightening on the steering wheel.

'We remember, Daddy,' they chimed together.

River gripped his twin's hand. 'I'll never let anything happen to Skye. She's our future.'

'So are you, my precious little man,' Ivy said. 'Don't forget that.' She reached back, touched both their precious faces.

'I won't, Mummy.'

A lightning bolt lit up the road ahead of them. Skye screamed as Paul jerked the car, trying to avoid the blast. Another and another hit the road in front of the car, beside it, until …

She was thrust out of the vision, panting, disoriented.

'Are you okay, Ivy?' Paul gripped her shoulders, holding her steady.

She looked up at him. 'That's the one,' Ivy said despite the horror of the crash, of what came after as the twins were taken and both Ivy and Paul died, their bodies disintegrating in the explosion that lit the night sky. It was worse than any other vision, so filled with trauma, but still, 'It's the one we have to choose.'

Paul stared at her, his eyes shadowed. 'Why would you choose that one. The way you die—'

'It doesn't matter. We have children,' she replied, wiggling her fingers in the swirling pool, manually backing up the image to show the two beautiful, bright faces in the back of the car. They looked like they were about ten. They had her nose and mouth and the shape of her eyes if not their colour and shared Paul's hair and the square determination of his jaw. The boy was most definitely a Were and the girl was a witch, but there was so much power shared between them it sizzled through the vision, stealing her breath. 'So strong. So essential. They are important, Paul. More important than anything. Can you feel it?'

He nodded, his eyes filling with awe as he stared at the children that would be theirs. Children they'd made together. The ones the pack had been waiting for to save them.

'They only appear in this future,' he said slowly.

She realised he was right. There was no sign of children in any other future—they, without exception, had shown them anywhere between a few months and a few years ahead, just the two of them, dying, no chance to have children.

This one was unique in two remarkable ways. Not only did this future give them children, it looked like it gave them much more time. It could take a mated pair—especially when they were not both Were—five to ten years to procreate.

'When does this take place?' she asked, excitement gripping her, thrusting away the horror of seeing all the deaths.

He tipped his head, weaving his fingers, moving the vision around to try to help answer her question. The image stilled on the phone in Ivy's lap—she'd never seen anything like it—then on the strange combinations of letters and numbers on the number plate of the car. 'It has to be many years from now.'

He nodded. 'They look about ten and we look like we're in our late thirties or early forties. Which gives us maybe twenty years together.'

She gripped his hand tighter, tears starring her vision as she looked at the image he'd stopped on of their children, so beautiful, determined and calm in the face of such stress. 'Twenty happy years together where we get to rear those two special people for ten years.'

'It's not enough,' he said.

'Of course it isn't. But it's more than I imagined. More than any other vision gives us by a long way.'

'But the children, they're so scared.'

She turned to him, gripped his other hand. 'I know. But they're alive. And we can find a way to make sure they are kept safe beyond our time with them. Your mother is there.' She pointed at one of the dark figures who arrived to fight the attackers who'd made the car crash. 'And your father.'

He stared at the image. 'But they're dead.'

'Not according to this.'

He nodded slowly. 'I've never had a vision that showed me her before, but I knew ...' He clenched his fist over his chest. 'Knew in here that no matter what Aunt Iris said, my parents weren't dead.

Knew she still had some significant role to play in my future. I could never stop thinking about her. Maybe this is why.'

'Maybe you're right.' She put her hand over his fist, stroking his fingers until they uncurled from the fist he'd made and twined with hers. 'When we study this vision to help us figure out what is happening and how we can help our children survive this inevitability, we might learn what happened to your parents all those years ago.'

'Maybe.' He met her gaze and stroked her hair back, his eyes starting to fill with bright hope. 'Although, the important thing is to make certain our children are prepared in every way possible to cope with this future without burdening them with it.'

'Yes. And we have twenty years to do it. Twenty years together. Ten of them raising our beautiful boy and girl. A Were and a witch. Both of them the hope for the future. I'm more than happy with that, my love. Are you?'

He stared into her eyes for long moments before placing a sweet kiss on her lips. 'Yes. I am.'

'Then what do we need to do to make certain this future is ours?'

He cycled back along the thread, too fast to see much more than the sense that despite times of worry and doubt, they had happiness, laughter and love as they explored their relationship and built their little family, surrounded by family, pack and friendships that only strengthened through the years.

Then he came to the moment that would set them along this path. It was as simple as starting their mating in the Goddess's place under the tree of memories she'd made for them. Then make love again under the moon and the stars on their hill in their timeline.

'Are you ready, my love?'

'Always,' she said.

13

He took her up and out of the vision place.

They opened their eyes, and smiled at each other.

The golden and amber leaves chimed a song of joy above their heads as they clasped hands and murmured, 'I accept you. You are mine.'

Paul bent his head as Ivy reached up for him. Their lips met and light flared, vibrant gold and silver, fracturing into all the colours of the spectrum as it hit the leaves above them and the grass under their feet. The light wrapped around them, lifting them up, then laying them down, not on the grass, but on a soft bed that had suddenly appeared for them.

Ivy pulled back from the kiss to laugh her delight. 'Magical.'

'Yes. You are,' he said, then kissed her again.

As he did, the broken threads of their mating bond uncurled, reaching out for each other, snapping into place one after the other as she wound her arms around his neck, returning his kiss. He pulled her closer, needing to feel her with every part of himself.

She furrowed her fingers into his hair, tightened her hold, then rolled over so she was on top of him, her body sliding along his. 'You're mine,' she growled, biting his lip.

He laughed with delight at her play, pulling back to see the wolf in her eyes. 'I love you too,' he said to her wolf and he could have sworn the wolf smiled back at him. Then she was kissing him again, her lips moving from his mouth, across his chin and down his neck, licking and sucking and biting.

It felt so good. It felt so right. Better than anything he'd ever felt before. Their touch, their closeness, mended what he had broken.

One by one, as hands pushed aside clothing and fingers ran over bare skin, the threads of the mating bond fluttered open from where they'd been curled, dead and almost lifeless inside him, inside her. They uncurled and straightened and reached, connecting, getting stronger and stronger with every touch, every kiss, every breath.

He flipped her over onto her back, drinking in her laugh and returned her playful growl. 'My turn,' he said. He ran his hand over her breast and a strand clicked into place, strengthening with every moan of encouragement she gave him. He bent down and replaced his hand with his lips, sucking her nipple into his mouth and swirling with his tongue. Her fingers dug into the muscles on his back, fingernails digging in, making him growl against her skin. Heat flooded across her skin and into him and another bond clicked into place.

He gave his attention to her other breast filling himself with her sounds and moans, the way her fingers scrabbled at his back, gripping tight. He didn't think he'd ever been this turned on, his cock so thick and tight it was almost painful. But he wasn't done with her yet. He needed to touch and taste all of her, bring her to orgasm with his hands and mouth before he had his fill.

He made his way down her stomach, hands and lips stroking over silky skin, fingers delving into the curls at the juncture of her legs.

'Paul,' she gasped. 'Please.'

He smiled a wicked smile he'd never felt on his lips before, then parting her, licked her long and hard. She was so sweet, so wet, her honey and spice taste coating his tongue, the spicy scent of her musk winding around him, a spell all of its own.

Her fingers scrabbled at his shoulders, moved into his hair, tightening in the curls as he licked and sucked and pushed two fingers deep inside her.

She cried out, a bell-peal in the floral scented air. The leaves above them picked up her cry and returned it to them in a musical peel. Her fingers in his hair, her desperate pants and moans, the way her body writhed under his merciless onslaught, drove him on. He didn't know how he knew to do this, what she would most like, but he was doing it and it filled him with such power, such strength of purpose, such confidence, that it felt like he was a master of making love to her. It didn't matter that he was a virgin—his responsibility to pack and his gift always coming between him and anyone he'd ever thought to be romantically interested in—he instinctively knew what would bring her pleasure, what to do, how far to push and he gave it his all.

Her back bowed and she gasped in a deep breath before crying out, her body vibrating and pulsing around his fingers, over and over. More threads of their bond clicked into place.

'Take me, take me now,' she said, panting hard as her body stopped vibrating and she fell back to the bed.

He rose over her. 'Are you certain?' Like him, she was a virgin too and he didn't wish to hurt her. He was so thick. So hard.

Her arms wound around him and she flipped him over and onto his back, her eyes full of vibrant passion, love and laughter. 'I have always been certain. I want you inside me, now. I need you inside me, now. Don't make me wait, my love.' And as she lowered herself on him, stretching around to accommodate him, he gripped her hips and pushed up into her slick, wet heat.

Bliss. Heaven. Peace. Happiness.

It surrounded him as she surrounded him. It was in her eyes as she looked into his. Their hands clasped; their breaths mingled. She stiffened as he broke through her barrier, holding still for a moment, but then she relaxed and moved on him. His eyes rolled into his head at the sensation, the friction, his balls tightening so much it was almost excruciating. He thought he was going to lose it, but her hands squeezed his and he forced himself to come back to her, looking into her eyes as she took him and he took her.

Together, they moved, creating a rhythm that was theirs, that echoed and vibrated on the air around them, causing the leaves to chime a new tune—their tune. One of happiness and completion.

'One. One. We are one,' they seemed to sing.

'You are mine,' she whispered as she moved over him, her body sinuous, strong.

'You are mine,' he whispered as he pushed into her, his body alive and stronger than it had ever been.

'Together.'

'Forever.'

Their pace quickened and sensation rose, magic prickling in the air around them, lifting them off the bed as they drove each other to completion.

Crying out, they shouted their joy to the sky, falling, falling ...

To land in the tall thick grass of his hill and complete their mating in their world and take those inexorable steps along the thread of fate they'd chosen.

Ivy was worried when they returned to the pack that their mating would horrify everyone. Paul had not been meant for her, but Fate had other ideas. She also wasn't certain which timeline everyone else would remember. How had their meddling with time and fate changed the world around them?

She shouldn't have worried. Nobody remembered what had occurred that day. Nobody remembered her illness. Time had returned to normal and the only ones with any memory of the change Paul had tried to make, were her and her mate.

Although, Iris and Abby looked at her in a way that made her think maybe they had a clue. They said nothing though, other than to give their approval to the mating that had occurred unexpectedly.

They were led to the Dance for the formal acceptance. The stones stood sentinel around them, holding the weight of ancient power—

having been brought here by the McVale Coven when they'd first arrived from Europe to claim this beautiful piece of land in the Peninsula near Red Hill, and make it their own. That power hummed around them, stroking over their skin, giving its own blessing to a union that the Fates had decreed, while they waited for the words of blessing and acceptance from their Alpha and their Coven Leader.

David McVale stared at them solemnly and Ivy trembled. Was her Alpha going to deny them a place in the pack as mates? It was unheard of for an Alpha to reject a mating, but she knew he had such plans for Paul and the strength Mariella would have brought to their pack. She wished she could tell him about Skye and River, but she and Paul had discussed it after completing their private mating, before heading back, hand in hand, to their families. They could not tell anyone else what lay ahead because the pack would try to stop it from happening and it couldn't be stopped. Couldn't be changed in any significant way. They also couldn't have their future children feel anything but the love and support of their pack—if the pack were worried about their future, they wouldn't be able to hide that worry from the children. It would affect everything, and they could not allow that to happen.

Skye and River must remember how much they were loved and feel the strength of connection and support if they were to get through what was ahead.

So, nobody could know how she and Paul would birth the future for their pack. And if David refused to welcome them as mates, then they would just have to live on the outskirts of the pack until the twins were born and they could show everyone the blessing their union brought.

She firmed herself against her Alpha's rejection, steeling herself for the hurt it would bring.

Then he smiled and held out his hands.

She took a breath for the first time since stepping into the circle and took his hand.

He placed Paul's hand over hers then encased them in both of his.

'Paul and Ivy have come to us today, once separate, now one.

Bonded as mates, heart and body, soul and mind, they are one. I accept their bonding into Pack McVale. May the strength of their mating strengthen our pack. From now and for all time.'

'From now and for all time,' the pack intoned.

'You are bonded before the Goddess and you are bonded before the pack. Let love fill your life and laughter fill your ears. May your arguments be short and your loving endless.' A few younger Were tittered at this part of the ceremony as they always did and there were the usual shushings and laughter. Ivy darted a glance to Paul and saw him sharing her smile. All nervousness was gone.

'May your love be eternal.'

'And may you find your eternal love,' the pack intoned, touching brow, lip and heart.

David beamed, lifting their hands. 'Ivy and Paul. Paul and Ivy. May you always be one.'

'One!" the pack shouted, their jubilation lifting on the air.

Paul grabbed Ivy up into a fierce hug, then met her seeking lips with his own. The heat of his kiss shot through her, making her tingle and fly up and up and up, but she wasn't lost, wasn't alone.

The pack drew them apart and into the celebration that seemed had been waiting for them. She danced with her mate then with her parents—they couldn't stop beaming at her, telling her that they'd always known she was the one to calm and settle Paul and make him happy. She danced with Stellan and Luke and Jackson. They teased her and she laughed, not even caring when Luke wondered when Poison Ivy had turned into Hot Ivy as Paul whisked her away from his mate, unable to stay away and keep his hands, and lips, off her. Which was fine with her.

She danced with Siobhan and Chloe, then laughed with everyone through Siobhan's speech, followed by Luke's as Paul's best man. Then Iris spoke followed by her parents and Stellan—she had no idea her brother had so many lovely things to say about her.

Then she danced with Paul again, her body plastered against his, moving as one.

The celebration raged around them, but every part of her was focused on one thing—Paul. Her wolf lolled inside her, blissful and content. But she suddenly needed to be alone with her mate.

One glance in his eyes had him nodding and taking her hand. They walked away from the circle and towards the cottage that would temporarily be theirs until a larger one had been built—the Pack Warlock must have the ability to entertain his pack, so a small cottage would not do.

But for now, it was perfect in every way.

Someone must have been in there earlier setting it up for the newly-mated couple. There was champagne chilling in a bucket on the table, and flowers everywhere. They walked upstairs and into the bedroom, which had been turned into the perfect lovers' bower—the king-sized bed covered with rose petals and plush pillows, gauzy curtains at the windows fluttering in the breeze coming up from the sea and everything done in her favourite colours—those she saw when she looked into Paul's brilliant blue eyes with their flecks of silver and green.

She reached for him as he reached for her. Their clothing melted away and then they were on the bed, skin sliding against skin, hands touching, desire rising, mouths tasting and teasing. Then she rose up, Paul with her and slid down onto the thick length of him. Breaths mingling, gazes tangled, they moved together, rising up and up until they both shouted their joy and jubilation to the sky, her wolf joining their happiness with a howl of pure joy in their minds.

They were accepted by their pack.

They were together as one.

They had time. They would have children.

They were blessed in so many ways. She looked into his eyes as they came down from the heights, smiling the wicked smile she would only ever smile for him and said, 'I am looking forward to our future.'

He returned her wicked smile. 'Me too, my love. Me too.'

Then he kissed her and showed her how much.

14

'I told you she would find a way.' Arianrhod turned to Morghanna as the ghost of the ancient witch came to stand beside her.

The Goddess nodded at her partner in this war she was fighting against the Darkness. 'It seems your faith in her was right.'

Morghanna smiled. 'Blood will out. She has much of Alistair in her. My love was always so strong.'

'And he has both you and your sister in him. It could have been a recipe for disaster trusting in them to find the way.'

Morghanna looked up at Arianrhod. 'Your worry surprised me, I have to say. I thought this path was one of the things you were certain about.'

Arianrhod turned from the shimmering pool in front of her, swiping her hand across the image of Paul and Ivy and their loving. 'It was the path I wanted them to choose. The path that needed to be chosen. But it was by no means certain they would choose it.'

'Then why did you let Paul try to change his fate?'

Arianrhod sighed. 'Because their choices make them stronger, as your choices made you stronger. I need strong soldiers for the fight ahead.'

'It's close now, isn't it?' Morghanna asked.

Arianrhod stared into the distance, across the sea she had created to look so much like the one Pack McVale's lands bounded. The choice to have them move across the ocean to this place so many years ago seemed so clear, but now so much of the path ahead was dark to her. Even so, she knew the end was closing in. She felt it in her bones. 'It is.'

'You still cannot see the outcome?'

'No. It is not something I can see.' Not something she wanted to see. She was not strong enough to see a future where she possibly didn't prevail against her old enemy.

It was strange to realise she wasn't as strong as the Were, witches and warlocks she'd worked with and manipulated down through the centuries, starting with Morghanna and down the generations to these two whose role was so important in what was to come.

This Were and warlock who were so special, they looked their deaths in the face and saw life and hope for the future.

It was remarkable. They were remarkable. 'Morghanna, I make a vow.'

'Yes?' Her friend, her servant, her partner, turned to her, brow raised.

'I vow as I did for you and your Alistair, to find a way to make certain Ivy and Paul's souls find a full life of love and commitment with each other in the future. When we win against the Darkness, I will make sure they are awarded this gift for their sacrifice.'

'That is very kind, my Goddess.'

Arianrhod shook her head. Once she might have been proud of her benevolence, but now, after centuries of working with Were, witches and warlocks in her endless machinations to beat the Darkness, she did not think in the same way as she once had.

Was she becoming a little more like those she once helped create? Perhaps.

She looked at the ghost of the woman beside her, so steadfast in her commitment to the cause and to right the wrong she'd once wrought. As strong as the two they'd just helped to set on a path to the end. 'No, not kind,' she whispered, thinking about what was to come. 'It is only right.'

―――――

ENJOYED *WITCH BOUND?* Want to find out what happens to Ivy and Paul's children and Arianrhod's plans for the Darkness? Follow the saga in the **Pack Bound Series.** Read on for the first chapter of Pack Bound: Book I.

PACK BOUND

PACK BOUND SERIES: BOOK 1

THE CURSE OF
MORGHANNA CANTRAE

T curse you, my pack, to a life without magic. May the right to change
be taken from you, your animals gaoled and tortured inside your
flesh as I have been gaoled and tortured inside mine. I curse you to
the eternal damnation of your kind. And I curse all others who let this
insanity befall one in their care. Take warning, from these, my last words,
all you who would come after: Look to the wellbeing of your Pack Witch or
suffer the fate of the MacCraes.

I tie my curse unto my death,
I curse you all with dying breath
Three times three times three times three
My will be done, so mote it be.

**Curse as transcribed by Father Luke as Morghanna was burned at
the stake for witchcraft, 1502, Edinburgh, Scotland.**

1

Skye stopped at the crest of the ski run and took a moment to appreciate the beauty of the Victorian Alps laid out before her. A breeze, full of the scent of eucalypts and the cool freshness of snow, blew a lock of red hair into her eyes. She swept it back under her ski hat and took a deep breath.

'What a beautiful day.' She'd skied in Austria and Canada, but even though the ski season was so much shorter in Australia and the snow not nearly as good, there was nothing like the stark beauty of the blue-tinged mountains of the Great Dividing Range. The other ski resorts were breathtaking too, but these mountains were home. They sang to her soul in a way the others couldn't.

Taking another deep breath, she pushed off over the crest and, with a wild 'Yahoo!', flew down the slope, her knees moving like rubber pistons as she attacked the moguls.

She ignored the swish and slide of other skiers around her, enjoying this moment of freedom on her last day, before she had to go back and face the real world. She wished she had an extra few days to gird her loins—as her grandpa used to say—against the responsibilities awaiting her at home, but it wasn't to be.

Instead, she was determined just to be happy with the now. It was a rare clear day at Mt Buller, and she was going to enjoy it to her fill.

She was just getting into a rhythm on the moguls when a strange chill crept down her spine—the kind of chill you got when someone was watching you surreptitiously. She'd been having that feeling off and on all day. She slowed, turning to see if she could catch them at it.

'Whoa!' she heard. Then something hard and heavy smashed into her. The sky tipped and an *oof* of breath exploded out of her as she hit the snow. A large body landed on top of her and then they were sliding, smashing over and through the moguls, until they finally slowed and came to a stop.

Head spinning, she lay with her arms flung out wide, crushed under the hot weight of a man. She moaned.

'Are you okay?' the man's husky voice murmured in Skye's ear.

'Only if I don't breathe,' she managed, surprised she wasn't winded. Snow inched into the collar of her parka. She shivered.

He shifted, pushing up onto his elbows to look down at her.

Despite the pain sparking through her body—damn, she was going to have some impressive bruises for show-and-tell on Monday —she became uncomfortably aware of the way their hips pressed together, legs tangled. She hadn't been this close to a man in way too long. This wasn't the way she'd imagined it happening again, though.

She tried to move. The action made his board—amazingly still attached to his feet—cut into her leg. She winced. 'Well, this is a very charming way to meet and all, but can you get off, please? You're crushing my legs.'

'Sorry.' He scrambled back.

'Oh, fudgy-duck!' She gasped as his board scraped over the bruise.

'Are you hurt?' He ran his hand over her leg, checking for injury.

Shivers chased across her skin that had nothing to do with the snow melting inside her jacket. Skye pulled away. 'No. I'm fine. Just let me stretch it out.'

He shifted back. But instead of getting up and skiing off like most other people would, he stayed, kneeling beside her as she stretched out her leg.

'I'm so sorry. I usually ski, but my brother talked me into trying out a snowboard this year.'

Her temper spiked at his words. Rubbing her aching leg, she snapped, 'Are you kidding me? What the hell are you doing on Federation? It's a black run—or didn't you notice all the signs up the top, you irresponsible arse?'

His eyebrows rose above his sunglasses. 'Wow. That thing about redheads and tempers is true.'

She bristled. 'You could have killed yourself, or someone else. Namely me!'

He brushed snow from his hair. 'For your information, I was doing okay until I hit that goddamned icy patch. I don't know why I agreed to try a board,' he grumbled.

He sounded so much like her twin, River, when he was pouting, that her flare of anger disappeared and she had to hide her grin. 'So why did you go over to the dark side?'

'My trickster of a brother said it would be a rush, but I think he just wanted to see me fall on my arse.'

Her lips twitched. 'That would be okay, except for the fact that you fell on mine.'

'It looked softer than mine.'

She choked on a laugh. 'Are you saying I have a fat arse?'

Rather than trying to back-pedal, his mouth curled into a lopsided smile—such a lovely mouth. 'No. In fact, I was thinking how nice it looked before I smacked into you.'

Skye dragged her eyes from his mouth. 'Is that why you took me for a toboggan ride, with me as the toboggan? To meet me and my nice arse?'

'That, and the fact you stopped so suddenly.'

She snorted. 'I thought you said there was an icy patch.'

'Yeah.' He laughed. 'I did. Didn't I?' He pushed his sunglasses off his face to look down at her.

She gaped.

He had the most startling eyes. They were deeply blue on the edge, almost black, but lightened to an icy blue at their centre. Lightning-bolt striations crazed through the iris, making it seem as if his eyes glowed. They reminded her of a picture of a wolf River had put on his bedroom wall when they were young. She'd asked him to take it down. He'd thought it was because she was frightened of big dogs, but it hadn't just been that. The wolf's eyes had haunted her in a way that confused her ten-year-old soul.

This man's eyes were even more dangerous to her equilibrium. They pulled her in. Her chest ached like she'd been winded.

He broke eye contact and pushed to his feet, allowing her to catch her breath. 'Here, let me help you up.' He put out his hand.

Don't touch him!

Skye hesitated as her inner voice barked at her; it was part of a spell her grandpa had woven to stop her from using her magic and to warn of any other magic users around. It usually sounded like her grandpa, calm and kind and supportive, but now her grandpa's voice held a tone like that of her grandmother, Morrigan Cantrae, at her commanding best.

Her first instinct was to do the opposite of anything Morrigan commanded. But she was no longer a child and instead of fighting it, she hesitated as she thought it through.

Her inner voice, changed or not, was only supposed to react so forcefully if she tried to use her magic—something that could never be allowed—or if an equally powerful witch or warlock was around or she was in danger.

Well, she hadn't used her magic and there was nothing about this man that suggested

he was a warlock; no tingling under her skin that warned her a true magic user stood before her. No sense of impending disaster.

And the chance of him being an axe murderer was pretty well zip.

So, if he wasn't a warlock or an axe murderer, there was no reason not to accept his offer of help.

She put her hand in his.

His fingers were strong as they wrapped around hers, and so warm the heat of him soaked into her, even through her gloves.

'Thanks,' she choked out as that warmth slid through her, doing something entirely untoward to her nerves. Overwhelmed, she pulled her hand from his grip.

He stepped back.

Perversely, now that he'd moved away, she wanted to get closer, beg him to touch her again. What the hell?

'Are you sure I can't do anything for you?'

Looking up into his face and those remarkable eyes, his voice a melting tenor in her ears, she forgot all about the pain in her leg and ankle. 'I'm pretty certain there are many and various things you could do for me.' Oh God! Had she said that out loud? She slapped her hand over her mouth, eyes wide. The look on his face told her she had. 'I'm sorry,' she muttered through her fingers. 'I don't know why I said that.'

He moved closer. 'I don't mind that you did.'

She swallowed hard, forced herself to answer. 'But I do. I don't know what's wrong with me.'

His brow furrowed again. 'Maybe you knocked your head.'

'I don't think so.' She tried to look away but couldn't. It was those eyes. And his voice. That was why she was behaving like such a weirdo. There was one room in the house where eyes and a voice like that really came into their own—and it wasn't the kitchen.

He was so gorgeous, with sinfully long dark lashes, the chiselled features of a male model and a dimple in his left cheek. The only thing that marred his perfect good looks was the scar that ran through his top lip—but that just made him look rugged and tough rather than pretty.

She sighed, wanting to touch his dimple, run her fingers across the stubborn jut of his jaw and linger on that scar. She wanted to flirt and have some fun. This was her holiday, after all. But she was vastly out of practice with flirting. She hadn't been on a date for years. What was the point when she could never get serious with anyone? Instead, she'd concentrated on building her business and spending time with River. Not that she minded: it was her fault her twin was housebound. She owed it to him to always be there.

The man stepped closer bringing her attention snapping back to him. 'Are you sure you're okay?'

The more he spoke, the more she thought of a good bottle of red, low seductive music and a plush fur rug before a fire. It was difficult not to reach for him, push her fingers through his silky brown hair and bring her lips to his.

But the way he looked at her indicated he didn't have the same inclination, regardless of his comments about her nice arse. He looked more confused than interested.

Disappointed when she knew she shouldn't be, she said, 'I'm fine, really.' She put weight on her sore foot and took a few hobbling steps. 'Almost as good as new.'

He looked unconvinced. 'Perhaps you should call it a day. You're limping.'

She shook her head. 'Are you kidding? It's not often you get days like this at Buller.'

She gestured at the blue sky, the snow-laden trees lining the run, the mountains of the Victorian Alps marching into the distance, covered in the blue haze of thousands of eucalypts. 'You would have to chop my leg off with your snowboard to stop me from skiing on such a beautiful day.' She cocked her head to the side, considering. 'Nah. Maybe not even then.'

He laughed, the sound washing over her like warm water lapping at her skin. 'Let me see you down to the bottom at least, make sure you get to the lift.'

Skye's gaze raked over his face, her vision blurring. The way he looked at her reminded her of something ... someone.

'Hello!' He waved his hand in front of her face. 'Don't tell me I gave you a concussion.'

She squeezed her eyes shut and shook her head. 'No. I'm fine. Just a bit of snow blindness.' Pathetic excuse, but with him standing so close, she couldn't seem to do better. Opening her eyes, she squinted. 'It's a bit bright with the sun. I should have worn my goggles.'

'Are you sure?'

His voice was hypnotic. She couldn't stop herself leaning forward, breathing in his scent. The need to give in to the temptation to touch, to kiss, to lick, was overwhelming. It was like she'd been bewitched.

She snapped upright. Panic clawed at her throat. Could she be? Bewitched?

No. Bron had said she had stronger shields than anyone she'd ever met, thanks to her grandpa's spell, and there was no reason not to trust her best friend in this matter. She was Wiccan after all. Not a true magic user like her family had been, but she did know about this stuff.

So what was happening to her?

Lust.

Yes. That was it. Mr Too-Gorgeous-For-Sanity was a fantasy come to life. She had to ignore the sensations shooting through her body. Force herself to be sensible. He was just being friendly because he'd knocked her over. And she'd made enough of a fool of herself for one day.

Biting her lip, trying to shelve her disappointment, she nodded. 'I'm sure. Go and kill your brother for making you snowboard and then enjoy the day.'

He chuckled. 'I might just do that. Adam needs a good killing.'

'Excellent. So, off you go. I'll be fine by myself.' Before he could say anything else, she hobbled down the hill to her skis. She clicked into the bindings, swallowing a gasp as pain sliced up from her ankle. Clenching her jaw, she endeavoured to ignore it. After all, she'd put up with worse.

There was the slide of board on snow behind her and she looked up to see the Adonis making his way down the slope towards her.

'How about I shout you a hot chocolate at Koflers just to make sure you're fine?'

Surprisingly pleased by his perseverance, Skye opened her mouth to say yes.

Don't say it! her inner voice snapped.

Taken aback, she blinked. *Why?*

He may not stink of magic, but there's something about him that's affecting you. Think about River. Think about what your magic did to him.

Even though the voice still didn't sound like it usually did, Skye knew it was right. This man might not have the magic to bewitch her, but he *was* making her behave strangely, almost to the point of acting without thinking—which she never did. She could never afford to lose control—her magic had only ever brought pain. She swallowed hard, knowing that despite the fact this was a holiday and she should be able to flirt and have fun, she couldn't do it with this man.

Taking herself in hand, she said, 'Thanks, but no thanks. I still want to get a few runs in before I call it a day.'

'What about a drink after? I feel I need to say sorry in some way.'

The wish to say yes was almost a pain inside her; but that in itself was reason to say no. 'I can't. I've got a prior engagement with friends.'

'I'm sorry to hear that.' He flashed a grin so charming it made her breath catch. 'I'll just have to hope we'll meet another time and your answer will be different.' He leaned forward, his astonishing warmth radiating towards her, and took a deep breath as if trying to breathe her in.

It was weird and yet ... unbelievably sexy.

'Okay,' she squeaked. Unable to stand his closeness for another moment and not give in to his invitation, she pushed off with her good leg and took off down the slope. Pain stabbed up her leg from her wounded ankle. A little whimper escaped from her lips.

What are you? A lion or a mouse?

A lion.

So ignore it. You have to get away from him.

She took in a shuddering breath—duck-it, she could still smell the warm male scent of him; earthy and yet clear and fresh, like the mountain air, yet so very different in how it affected her. Mountain air was cooling, refreshing; this was ... hot and made need simmer under her skin. She took in another breath as she created more distance between them; but the scent stayed with her as if it was imprinted on her senses.

A tingle started down her spine. Was he watching her? Were his eyes caressing her arse the way he said they had been before he crashed into her? She almost groaned at the memory of the way they'd come to a stop, his body spread on top of hers, chest to chest, legs tangled. Skye bit her lip as muscles well below her abdomen clenched and quivered.

It was a sensation she'd not felt for a long time—too long. Hell, she'd almost become a nun with the length of time she'd been celibate, and she'd been content with that. But coming face to face with that Adonis would make even a nun change her habits. It wasn't so unusual that he'd had such an impact on her.

Or was it?

She stopped herself from glancing back over her shoulder. It didn't matter what she felt. All that mattered was it couldn't be. Her life was like this by necessity. There was no choice. She'd come to terms with that a long time ago.

Lifting her face to the sun, she decided to luxuriate in the rare spring day and not worry about could-have-beens.

The sapphire blue sky was glorious.

And reminded her of his eyes.

She stared at the choppy snow in front of her. Yes, that was better. Nothing about the snow reminded her of him. It did remind her that she needed to thank Shelley and Bron once again for agreeing to change their plans for a Noosa holiday and had come with her to Mt Buller instead for the last of the season. Good snow in spring was a rarity, so she hadn't been able to pass up the opportunity when a few days before they were due to leave for Noosa, a huge dump was reported. Fresh powder, the blue skies of spring and the freedom she only felt in the mountains was a siren call she couldn't ignore. Thankfully her friends agreed, even though they weren't as keen to get on the slopes as she was and stay there all day. They were more into staying at the lodge or enjoying a cocktail or two at one of the bars that was still open at this time of the year.

Which was where she'd left them to come out and get in a few more runs before the lifts closed for the day.

They had planned to go out again tonight for their last night here and she'd been looking forward to it, but the pain in her ankle was beginning to make her doubt if she'd be able to. By the feel of it, she might have done some serious damage. Duck-it! Bron was bound to fuss and Shelley to lecture.

Her spine tingled again. Was Mr Too-Gorgeous-For-Sanity still watching her? She turned her head to sneak a peek and lost her rhythm. Her ski slid down the side of a mogul and pain jagged up her leg. She groaned.

'Are you okay?' he yelled, his voice winding around her like a feather stroke even at this distance.

She didn't look back again, only waved, hiding her red face, not wanting him to ski after her.

A moment later, she pulled up at the end of the queue of skiers and boarders waiting to get on the lift. She chanced a glance back up the slope. He stood right where she'd left him and something about the way he stood made her certain he was still looking right at her. She shivered, the sensation far too pleasurable for her own—or anyone's—good.

She shuffled forward, glad the queue was fast moving, but still she couldn't help breathing out a sigh of relief as she hopped on a chair and it climbed into the air through shielding trees.

Adonis might not be a warlock, but his combination of good looks, charm and velvety voice was just as dangerous. He'd not only made her want to change her nun-like habits, he made her feel like a horny teenager. He'd even made her consider, for a split second, turning her back on her obligations and the promises she'd made to her grandpa and to River.

She could never do that. Ever.

Those promises kept them all safe.

As the lift rose over the crest of the slope, she shivered. This time it wasn't the feeling of being watched that made that strange tingle race up and down her spine; thoughts of what happened all those years ago always did this. Her magic pushed at her, fighting to get out.

She swore, pushing it back down. That man's presence had addled her brain, made her shields weak. Closing her eyes, she repeated the mantra she'd been taught.

Her magic was dangerous. To protect River and everyone she loved, it was something she could never set free.

2

'Was that her?'

With a slide of board on snow, Adam came to a halt. Jason didn't turn to look at his brother, his gaze still on the place where the lithe redhead had disappeared as the chair she was on rose over the crest of the hill. Unexpected warmth still fired through his body.

'If that was her, why's she running away?' Adam clapped his brother on the shoulder.

'Did you try your charm on her?'

Jason didn't answer. His mind was too full of the woman: those green eyes like spring pools, glistening with hidden depths in the sun; her hair, licks of flame on her shoulders; her generous mouth full of laughter and mischief. Even that spike of temper and the funny way she'd had of swearing had been sexy.

Despite himself, he was engaged. He hadn't expected that. And her scent—his wolf had growled at her scent. Familiar, yet there was also something strange about it.

'Aren't you going to follow her?'

Jason shook his head and brushed the snow off his pants. 'No. Something's wrong. She didn't recognise what I am.'

'Maybe she isn't our Pack Witch.'

Jason clicked his boot onto the snowboard and balanced for a moment, shifting his weight back and forth. 'I'm pretty sure she is. But there's something ...' He shook his head. 'She should have expelled some magic when she saw me, but she didn't.'

Adam frowned and sniffed. 'But I can smell that zip in the air, like the electrical build-up before lightning. Doesn't that denote magic?'

Jason thought about the last time they'd encountered the scent of magic—the night their parents, two older brothers and their mates had been murdered in their never-ending quest to find their kidnapped Pack Witch. The scent in the air now, a scent that lingered in his nostrils like a teasing perfume, was nothing like that acrid scent. 'It is magic. But she didn't expel it when she saw me. It's around her all the time, like a cloak, but muted or something.' That was definitely wrong. Yet he was sure it was her. He'd seen her in his dreams; dreams he'd always had of her; dreams that had been nebulous things until the Calling had caught up with him after his father's murder and he'd become Alpha.

'How can you be certain it's her then?'

'Because of the dreams. I saw her skiing here with her friends.'

'You dragged us here to chase down a woman who doesn't even smell like she has the magic of a Pack Witch all because of some dreams?'

'They're not just dreams. It's the link.'

'What link?'

'The link between the Alpha and the Pack Witch. Dad was linked to Paul Collins—'

'As Iris Collins was linked to Grandpa before him.'

'Yes.' It was the only way the magic worked. The Pack Witch fed it into the Alpha and the pack syphoned it from the Alpha through the Packbond—the ultimate form of synergy.

'But how are you linked to Paul's daughter?'

The question was understandable. A bonding wasn't supposed to be undertaken until a Pack Witch or Warlock was of age, after they'd imbibed the Bond Wine. But in this case ...

Jason looked out at the distant mountains. The moment he'd clapped eyes on her, he'd realised that Paul Collins had linked them all those years ago—the future Alpha and the future Pack Witch. It's why he'd had the dreams. It made sense of something that had always seemed nonsensical to him. Something he'd spent years denying because he'd been too young to understand the significance of what had been done to him. The proof was irrefutable though.

The link was the reason he'd found her when nobody else could.

'Paul linked us when Skylar was a few months old.'

'What?' Adam gripped his arm, his voice bitter. 'Did you keep this from me because I'm nothing but the Trickster?'

'No.' Jason clasped Adam's shoulder. 'And don't talk like that about yourself. From what I've been reading in the Pack Witch Diaries, the Trickster is far more essential to a pack than we remember. Besides, I have named you my second. I wouldn't keep anything from you. It's just ... I've only now realised what Paul did.'

He remembered standing in the dark room looking down at her crib, Paul lighting candles that had smelled like jasmine and cinnamon and honey. He'd muttered words Jason hadn't understood and in the quiet hush that followed, a sizzle had shot along Jason's skin, sinking into his nerve-ends and sparking in his brain. The baby had cried out, holding out her chubby little arms to him. Despite being a boy who thought babies were smelly, noisy things, he'd picked her up, bouncing her until she giggled. That giggle had fizzled inside him like popping candy, leaving him with the same sense of warmth and sweet aftertaste.

'It is done. You will keep my daughter safe,' Paul had whispered.

Jason hadn't realised the significance. He'd just been a small boy holding a pretty baby who smelled of powder and her mother's sweet milk.

'Why would he do that when it goes against pack law?'

Jason was brought out of his reverie by his brother's question. He understood the horror in Adam's tone. The pack's greatest duty was to look after their children. They would never do anything to hurt or place unnecessary burden on a child. But Paul had done exactly that when he'd linked Skylar to Jason.

'He was prescient. Maybe he'd seen this future. Maybe he knew I would become

Alpha and that I would have to find her.'

Adam shook his head. 'I always thought Paul looked sad. It's no wonder if this is what he saw.'

Jason glanced at his brother and sighed at the look of devastation on his face. Nobody would have looked at Paul and thought him sad, yet Adam had seen beyond the facade Paul showed to the world, to the grief of a man who saw things he shouldn't. It was remarkable sometimes, the things the Trickster saw. Things none of them had realised the significance of until it was almost too late. Now he knew that without Adam pushing fun and laughter into the Packbond, the pack would already have succumbed to the Curse. He'd maintained positivity when there was nothing to be positive about.

And it was taking a toll. As Alpha, linked to his brother in ways he'd never been linked before, Jason could feel the pressure of pack wellbeing tear at Adam. He wished he could take some of that burden but it wasn't possible. Not until they had their Pack Witch back safe and sound and the Curse averted. Because, more than anything, he knew that what Adam was doing for the pack was helping to keep him from slipping into deadly insanity.

Gripping his brother's shoulder, Jason whispered, 'I know. I know the burden that knowledge places on you.'

Adam swallowed hard. 'I know you do.' He gripped Jason's shoulder in turn. 'That's why you make one fucking great Alpha.'

Jason smiled and slapped his brother on the arm. Even when torn apart by a pain that wasn't his, Adam couldn't help but see the bright side. 'I think you're right about Paul. He saw at least some part of the future. That's why he linked Skylar and me at an age when it would normally be forbidden.'

'Did Mum and Dad know?'

Jason frowned. 'I think perhaps they did, after the fact. Why else would they have given me such freedom?'

'Because they were sick of listening to you whinge and whine about wanting choice,' Adam said. He managed to keep a straight face when Jason glared at him, then burst out laughing.

Jason chuckled 'You can't help yourself can you?'

'Comes with the burden of being the funny one.'

'You're funny, all right,' Jason said, twirling his finger beside his head.

'You can talk. I'm not the one following strange dreams.'

'You're right.' Jason sighed, all levity dying as his thoughts turned darker. 'I just wish the link had activated properly before Mum and Dad, Seamus and Sian, and Josef and Marianne were killed.'

'But that's not how it works.'

'No. Dad had to die for me to find her.' He ground his board into the snow, fingers clenched, the wolf desperate to break through and claw at something.

'You can't blame yourself for that. You didn't kill them.'

Jason's lips curled into a snarl. 'No. I didn't. But I swear by the Dark Moon, I will find who did.'

It all came down to the woman he'd just smashed into: Skylar Collins.

She was their hope of a future without madness. She was also the only hope he had of finding those responsible for causing the Curse to touch his pack, bringing them to near extinction.

'So, if that is Skylar, why didn't she use her magic when she saw you?'

Jason took in a deep breath of clear, cool air, trying to calm himself. 'I don't know. But I have no doubt that the reason why Cordelia or the old McClune Pack Witch could never scry for her is at the heart of it. Whoever took her hid her by changing more than her name.'

'So, what's the plan?'

'I'm going to bump into her again at the lodge and when the time's right, I'm going to share some wine with her.'

Adam's eyes glittered with understanding. 'Do you think crashing into her was the best way of meeting her then? I don't know if she'll want to share the Bond Wine with an accident-prone idiot.'

As was the Trickster way, Adam was trying to lighten his mood. It worked. Jason's lips split into a grin. 'I didn't think she'd stop short like that, but in retrospect it was a stroke of genius. Because if she heals herself, we'll know there isn't anything wrong with her magic. Besides, I got so close, I filled myself with her fresh scent. I can track her anywhere now.'

'Will that be necessary?'

'We'll see. But at least we know she can't disappear again. It's taken too long to track her down. I don't want to waste any more time.'

'I'm with you there. I'm sick of this.'

The growl in his brother's tone had Jason's gaze sliding to Adam. There was a red tinge in the amber of his eyes. The darkness Adam had banished moments ago had returned. Ultimately, breaking the Curse would cure that, but for now ... 'You need to hunt.'

'Later. Let's race.'

With a whoop, Adam took off down the slope, his motions balletic as he controlled the board. Jason's smile widened into a thoroughly wolfish grin as he caught Skylar's scent; still clear even though she'd was gone. His wolf wanted to hunt her down right now—it didn't like that she had run from them.

Soon, he promised, stroking his wolf with a mental hand. *For now, let's go chase Adam.*

The wolf growled its agreement.

Pushing forward, he followed Adam down the slope, catching air as he flew over a snow-capped boulder and cut Adam off. He heard Adam's bark of laughter as his brother tried to push past him; a sound he echoed as he passed the Trickster in a few quick movements, beating him to the queue by a hairsbreadth.

Adam might have been doing this longer, but nobody beat Jason in the chase. And Skylar Collins was about to find out that running only served to sweeten the hunt.

I HOPE you enjoyed that sneak peek of *Pack Bound.* To read more, you can find all the buy links here:

https://www.leislleighton.com/paranormal-romance-novels/#packone

IF YOU DON'T WANT to miss out on news about the Dawn of the Curse Series (a Pack Bound Prequel Series) as well as special giveaways, sales, book signings and information on my other books, then sign up to my newsletter.

As an added bonus, when you join, you will get a FREE ebook copy of *Fractured Curse*, the prequel novella to my popular Gods Cursed Series. Turn the page to find out more ...

LOVE A FREE BOOK?

YOUR FREE BOOK IS WAITING

GET YOUR EXCLUSIVE PREQUEL TO THE GODS CURSED SERIES RIGHT HERE:

Cursed to never be loved; fated to never be alone ...

Cursed cupid Tamuel has been told he will never love or be loved, a fate to which he's long been resigned. Yet from the moment he meets powerful trainee witch Korinna Soteira at the Amazonian and Gargarean training camp, he knows this to be a lie – he loves Korinna like he's loved nothing and no-one in his life. But his curse is right in one respect: he may be able to love, but he can never *be* loved. Korinna will only ever be his friend, a fact he has spent the last twenty years coming to terms with.

However, malignant forces are stirring in the darkest reaches of the Realms. They have plans to use Korinna and her unusual powers – plans that can only be thwarted by the cursed cupid and an impossible love. Yet breaking Tamuel's curse now could release a force too ancient to destroy – and thus destroy any future.

What if the only way to survive the present is to place the future in peril?

Fractured Curse is a prequel novella to my popular Gods Cursed Series centring on unknown history between two of readers' favourite characters from the series. It takes place 2000 years before the events in *Love Cursed* and can be read as an introduction into the world or at any time during the reading of the series.

It's exclusive to my newsletter subscribers, so to get your copy, just follow the QR code or link below, fill in your details and it will be winging its way to you along with other free reads, deals and bookish info.

Get My Free Copy of Fractured Curse Here:
https://www.subscribepage.com/fracturedcurse_signup

JOIN LEISL'S LEGENDS

Subscribe to (or follow) me (via the QR code) at my Leisl's Legends page on REAM—a new subscription app like Patreon except it's designed especially for readers and authors for an amazing reading experience—and you will get early access to *The Huntress and the Vampire King,* my hot enemies to lovers, witch-and-vampire-licious urban fantasy romance that readers over there are already in love with. It's the prequel novel to the first book in the Blood-Rites Series - *The Blood of the Seer*.

Be the first to find out where it all began with Anita and Hei's love story.
BECOME A LEGEND NOW!
https://reamstories.com/leislleightonauthor

You will also find serialised chapters of the next book in my popular **Gods Cursed Series** there and can comment on the story as I write it! Not to mention you will also get extra bonuses like exclusive NSFW Bonus Epilogues, Bonus Prologues and cut scenes and chapters from all of my books.

Be part of creating the stories you love AND get exclusive access to a whole range of goodies including other WIPs, bonus content, voting rights, signed books and more.

Read on to find out more about The Huntress and the Vampire King PLUS read the opening chapters ...

The Huntress and the Vampire King

She hates the vampire who saved her; he holds the key to her fate ...

Hunter-witch Anita Middleton wants revenge against the violent vampire cults that murdered her father and has worked hard to become one of the best vampire hunters there is. But on a difficult hunt she is caught in an ambush and is mortally wounded ... only to be saved by a mysterious warrior. A warrior with brilliant blue eyes and long silver-blonde hair who fights with a grace and violence like nothing she's seen. It is only after she wakes in the heart of his palazzo that she realises her saviour is a vampire - and according to her brother and mentor, this vampire king is their ally.

Lord Hei rules over an empire of witches, humans and vampires who have been trying to keep the vicious vampire cults, the Wild and Dark Brethren, at bay for centuries. Then he saves Anita and knows with one look she is the prophecied Huntress who could be his downfall or his salvation - and she is also his fated mate. But she struggles to trust him as her hatred of vampires is deep-seated. And she *needs* to trust him because only he can offer the specialised training a Huntress needs so her power won't overwhelm her.

But with the Dark Brethren mysteriously amassing, he has little time to win her over. And Anita must go on a crash course to learn how to control her Huntress magic ... or go slowly and violently insane.

The Huntress and the Vampire King is the exciting action-packed prequel novel to *The Blood of the Seer*.

If you love your vampires hot with a bit of The Witcher thrown in and your heroines as kick-arse as Buffy and even more tortured, if you love fated mates, enemies to lovers, chosen ones and epically hot romance mixed with action and mystery, then *The Huntress and the Vampire King* is what you've been waiting for.

Sign up to Leisl's Legends and start reading exclusive early release chapters of it now!

BECOME A LEGEND NOW!
https://reamstories.com/leislleightonauthor

ALSO BY LEISL LEIGHTON

PACK BOUND SERIES

Pack Bound

Moon Bound

Shifter Bound

Wolf Bound

Witch Bound

(A Pack Bound Series Prequel Novella -

FREE ebook copy to Newsletter Subscribers)

BOX SET

Pack Bound Series Collection Books 1-4

DAWN OF THE CURSE
A PACK BOUND PREQUEL SERIES

Soul Bound

Alpha Bound

Hunter Bound

Fae Bound

(Coming in 2027)

GODS CURSED SERIES

A Love Cursed Christmas Wish

Love Cursed

Soul Cursed

Blood Cursed

Hearts Cursed

Fates Cursed

Witch Cursed

Dragon Cursed

(Coming 2026)

BLOOD-RITES SERIES

The Blood of the Seer

The Blood of the Sire

The Blood of the Son

(Coming 2027)

BLOOD-RITES PREQUEL AND BONUS MATERIAL

The Huntress and the Vampire King

The Middleton Manifesto

(Available now via Leisl's Legends subscription)

ANTHOLOGIES

A Perfectly Paranormal Valentine

A Perfectly Paranormal Halloween

A Perfectly Paranormal Easter

A Perfectly Paranormal Christmas

A Perfectly Paranormal Prophecy

(Coming in 2027)

As well as writing sexy, epic and romantic paranormal novels, I write mysterious and emotional romantic suspense novels too. Check out the following titles for amazing, suspenseful reads:

STORM HAVEN SERIES

Need You Tonight

The Devil Inside

COALCLIFF STUD SERIES

Climbing Fear: Book 1

Blazing Fear: Book 2

ECHO SPRINGS SERIES

Dangerous Echoes: Book 1

Books 2-4 in this series, (written by Daniel deLorne, TJ Hamilton and Shannon Curtis) are also available now at all ebook retailers.

You can find all the buy links for Leisl's Books at her website:

ABOUT LEISL

Leisl Leighton is a tall red head with an overly large imagination. As a child, she identified strongly with Anne of Green Gables, and like Anne, is a voracious reader and born performer.

It came as no surprise when she went on to a career as a performer, script writer, script doctor, stage manager and musical director for cabaret and theatre restaurants.

After starting a family, Leisl stopped performing and began writing the stories plaguing her dreams. She now writes emotional stories mixed with mystery and a little bit of what goes bump in the night.

Her novels have won and placed in writing contests here and overseas. She is a passionate advocate for the romance genre, was President of Romance Writers of Australia from 2014-2017 and when she's not writing romantic stories of redemption, she is helping other authors reach their dreams with her Author Services.
You can contact Leisl through her website via the QR Code above or here: https://www.leislleighton.com

And if you want to stay in touch and be the first to find out about new releases, appearances, special deals and exclusive content and give-

aways, sign up to her Newsletter and pick up your free copy of *Witch Bound* via the QR code.

Or sign up to *Leisl's Legends* via this QR code to get *Witch Cursed* plus serialised early access stories and bonus content including a bonus

NSFW ending for Love Cursed.

You can also follow her on social media:

facebook.com/LeislLeightonAuthor

instagram.com/leislleightonauthor

bookbub.com/authors/leisl-leighton

amazon.com/stores/Leisl-Leighton/author/B00DBYRGZY

ACKNOWLEDGMENTS

Thanks go to all the usual people: my hubby, my boys, my mum and dad, my writing group friends—Anita, Marnie, Chris, Laura, Frana— for all their love and support through the good and bad in this very terrible year.

Thanks to Helen and Liz—your council and amazing friendships will always be missed.

Thanks to my agent, Alex Adsett, for encouraging me to go off and pursue getting these stories out there myself.

Thanks to my editor, Brooke Halliwell—working with you is always a joy.

And thanks to the Fantasy Realms writers for letting me tag along and then encourage me to get this out into the world all on its lonesome. A more amazingly talented bunch of people I couldn't imagine, and to be included as one of you is an honour and a privilege. I hope to work again with you all in the future. An especially big thanks to Dan for asking me to come on board and Lana, not only for her 'hell-yeah, come join us,' but for her astonishing and eye-catching covers —Lana, your talent never ceases to take my breath away.

Finally, thanks to all the readers. I hope you enjoy our stories as much as we enjoyed writing them.

www.ingramcontent.com/pod-product-compliance
Lightning Source LLC
Chambersburg PA
CBHW070613120726
47909CB00004B/1202